THE FOUNDLING HOUSE

JOHN A. HODA

OLIVERHEBERBOOKS

The Foundling House 2026 © John A. Hoda

Cover design by Kim Killion

Published by Oliver-Heber Books

0 9 8 7 6 5 4 3 2 1

"What's that smell?" Alice peeks around me to look at the wicker basket Sally holds in the crook of her right arm. The dull flickering light in this alley shines from the streetlamps and the gin palaces along Commercial Street. It's a few minutes after midnight on an unseasonably warm late November night in Whitechapel. Illicit businesses catering to the carnal tastes of visitors are in full swing.

"Would you like a scone?" I pivot to allow Alice a closer look into Sally's basket. We inch towards the light in a practiced move. Sally and I have done this dance before with the women of the night who trade their bodies for gin.

"My mum taught us how to bake. Try one." Sally takes several steps closer to the main road, and Alice follows her nose.

She appears hesitant. "Are you sure, Francine?"

I nod, and Sally opens her basket. The smell of fresh baked goods wafts over us, temporarily replacing the smell of horse droppings on the street and urine sprayed on the walls by drunks too lazy to find a privy.

She takes a scone of her choice and samples it. "This is delicious." She blurts out before swallowing and taking another bite.

I produce a bottle of water from my basket and tell her to drink. She takes a swig and returns to her scone for a larger bite. Alice's grey frock and brown skirt have seen better days. Both are soiled from vomit and sleeping rough. I've watched her descend into hell for a couple of months now. Personal hygiene and eating regularly have been replaced by her slavery to the devil's drink. She eats in silence. I see real thirst and hunger returning to her.

Sally offers her another scone, and this one disappears as quickly as the first. She empties the first bottle of water and downs a second. Soon she will need to sleep off these treats.

"How would you like to sleep in a warm and clean bed and have proper a breakfast in the morning?" I ask on cue.

She looks at me warily. "What's it gonna cost? I've no money."

Sally answers first, "Nothing! Francine, do you think we have some spare clothes in the closet?"

I shrug my rehearsed shrug. "We will only know if she tries some on."

"My mum is coming over tomorrow to show us how to make beignets. They're French treats dusted with sugar. Would you like to watch?" Sally knows how to reel them in after I set the hook.

"I dunno. I have to give it a think. There's still time for me to get into the doss house." This tells me she has not paid for a week or even a day in advance. Even more important to have her come home with us. Home? I still have trouble thinking of the mansion on the other side of the Thames as home.

Just then, the skies let loose with fat raindrops. Sally and I open our large umbrellas and step back, leaving Alice to get drenched. We are helping her to decide in our favor. Heavy rains will discourage male visitors to Whitechapel looking for their carnal pleasure. We know it, and so does Alice.

We motion for her to join us. "The cab stand is over by the train station. Clean dry clothes and a warm bed beckon you," I say.

"I know what you are trying to do, Francine Murphy." She backs away from us. "I can take care of myself, thank you…"

We hear a woman's scream, not out of fear but from pain, further down the alley just past whence we once stood.

We peer into the darkness and strain our ears to hear over the rain pounding the cobblestones. This first burst of rain in several days has brought more ripe smells to our nostrils. It will be a few more hours before all the stench finds its way to the sewers and finally into the Thames.

"Is it the Ripper?" Alice shrieks. Her eyes bug open in terror.

Knowing better, I say, "No. Let's go investigate."

Alice's fear of a man slicing a woman apart is real. At least five women this summer and autumn fell victim to that madman in a multi-block square from where we stood. We scan the darkness. Nothing. No movement. No rats scurrying about. No cats chasing them. We spread out, looking into alcoves, behind wooden boxes and barrels. The rain subsides for a moment, and my straining ears pick up a loud sigh at the same moment Alice screams, "Over here!"

Movement emanates from under the skirt of a motionless woman lying on top of newspapers and rags under a slight overhang. The ground below is barely out of the rain.

"Dearie?" Alice asks.

The young woman doesn't stir. Her pale skin peeking from under her black bonnet is tinged blue. She is not breathing.

I shook her shoulders. She is warm to the touch. No response. Her head covering falls to the ground. Her blonde hair uncoils and splays out. I see no bleeding from her upper body.

Sally puts down the basket and gently reaches under the girl's skirt and pushes up the bodice to reveal a newborn with the cord wrapped tightly around its neck.

Alice retrieves a knife from her boot, grabs a handful of the slippery, bloody cord, makes it taut and cuts it. Her movements are quick and clean. Maybe in a previous life, she was a midwife.

Alice unwraps the cord from around the baby's neck. "There you go, baby girl. Breathe."

I scan the faces. The squished purplish-blue face of the baby remains still. Alice's furrowed brow tells me something is wrong with the infant. Sally's eyes dart back and forth to the unresponsive mother and baby.

I stare at the infant. My miscarriage leaps into my thoughts as the memory of the face of my baby I lost blurs into the face of the child in Alice's hands. She pinches the baby's tiny nose and blows a butterfly kiss into its mouth. She turns the baby over in her one hand and taps gently on her back. A slight tremor is followed by a convulsion as the infant expels mucous and placenta blood onto her mother's skirt. The baby cries out and takes a large breath. Alices uses her smallest finger to swab the baby's mouth and pulls out another thick gob, which pulls a thick string of mucus from the lungs. The baby's color is improving with each piercing cry.

"Here." Sally points to the basket. The soft blanket separating the temptations is inviting. The warm scones are arranged under the blanket. A makeshift bed is fashioned. "Shall we take her to Doctor Jekyll?"

"Alice, come with me. Sally go to the street and call out for help." I hand her a few coins. "For the ride back." Can I trust her not to use it for drinking after what she witnessed tonight? Doctor Jekyll is a benefactor to these women of the street whom I have taken in. He provides us with food, clothing and a clean house on Cavendish Square. For me to call it home is very complicated. But on a night like this, with what I just witnessed, I can let my guard down this once.

Sally had walked away from these streets and into my outstretched hands only a short while ago. This would be a test of her sobriety. Sally's mother saw Sally's progress and offered to bake for us. She comes by from time to time to teach us recipes. A handy skill to have, and we get to sample the bounty from our practice.

Alice touches the baby's tiny hand to her mother's lips. "A kiss from heaven. God rest her soul. She's already there."

We adjust her tired bodice and pull down her skirt to give her some dignity in this dimly lit alley on her bed of newspapers and rags, her last resting place.

With the baby in hand, Alice and I rush to the train station where the cabs queue; Sally runs back to Commercial Street. Good fortune is with me, and we hail a cab at the next intersection. Alice holds the basket with one arm as we bounce and jostle directly to Jekyll's address. I pay the fare while Alice bangs on the front door.

I hear Lucky, the dog who brought Doctor Henry Jekyll and me together, bark with ferocity, until I climb the steps to the front entrance. Upon hearing my voice, Lucky changes his tune. A bleary-eyed man of fifty-five years of age opens the door wide. He's tall with wide shoulders and black hair, standing barefoot and wearing nightclothes. I had never seen the good doctor so lightly dressed.

"The baby is having trouble breathing. The cord was wrapped tight around her neck, and I pulled some of the mucus out, but I didn't get it all, I'm afraid," Alice reports. A future Alice appears to me in this instant, not the gin-soaked prostitute trading sex for booze.

"Bring them to my examining room, Francine, while I change," Henry says.

2

What has Francine gotten me into? It's been at least three years since I practiced medicine. I can count on one hand the number of times I examined an infant. My patients before I fled London for the island were wealthy West End women in need when it was their time of the month. I also provided mentholated rubs for aches and pain, dispensing formulas for whatever ailed them. I sutured open wounds and set fractures for their employees. Earlier in my career, I had a surgery and performed many operations, but as Hyde became more active, I lost my nerve to cut open patients and defaulted to treating the well-heeled inhabitants of the West End. So much has happened since my return, but mostly I am struggling with who I've become.

I'm still recovering from that early morning awakening on the wharf in Francine's arms a fortnight past. Yes, she is Francine to me in private and Mrs. Murphy in public, and I am Henry and Doctor Jekyll to her in those situations. Our relationship is less formal now that she knows my secretiveness surrounding Edward Hyde.

She brought home an infant. I will find out how ill-prepared

I am for this examination. I finish washing the sleep from my eyes and rinsing soap from my hands and arms up to my elbows and hastily put on the shirt and trousers I wore that evening as they are close by. Preferring slippers to boots in my home, I slip them on and pad downstairs to the examination room.

I am greeted by the aroma of baked goods. My stomach growls involuntarily. The room is bright and warm. Louise, New Hope's housemother, walks in behind me with a tea set. New Hope is the name Francine settled on for her venture. Odd place and time for an impromptu party.

Francine and the other women peer into the oak slat basket from either side of the examination table. She says, "This is Alice. She found the mother and this baby. We are afraid that the mother died in childbirth. Sally remains in Whitechapel to see what can be done about the poor woman."

"As I told you, sir, the cord was tight around her neck, and I removed it. I could get her breathing, but she doesn't sound right." Alice's concern is etched on her furrowed brow and taut jawline.

"Lift her out of the basket gently," I tell her. Francine stands back as I attach my stethoscope to my ears. Alice removes the blanket swaddling the baby, and for the first time, I have a good look at the newborn. I press the cone gently on her chest. The heart beats with a strong steady rhythm; the lungs are obstructed with fluids. How much and how deep I am not sure.

My Potain aspirator has its own case, and I remove it from my visitation bag. I go to the cabinet, unlock it with the key that I only possess, and remove a bottle of alcohol and sanitize the suction tube. The bottle goes back into the cabinet, and I lock it up. No sense in creating more temptation for the women Francine and Louise walk out of hell.

"I have to be extremely careful to use the lightest touch, lest I implode the lungs. Could someone fetch me a basin of clean warm water?"

Louise runs toward the kitchen.

"Tell me what happened," I say.

Alice releases a torrent of information. There is no gin-talk. She appears sober. I wonder what condition Francine found her in. "...and we was talking on Commercial Street when suddenly we heard this god-awful scream down the alley. At first I thought it was Jack the Ripper taking apart another woman..."

Francine and I steal a quick glance.

"Anyway, Francine tells us not to imagine the worst, and we run down the alley, but we don't see the screaming woman anywhere."

Francine interrupts. "It stopped raining for a second, and I heard a loud sigh."

Alice says, "I musta been fifteen feet away from her when I heard it too. I called Francine and Sally over."

"We found a woman on her back. Her eyes were open and blank. She was still, not breathing, and she looked..." Francine turned her head away from us.

"Dead." Alice finished the sentence and added, "Something shifted between her legs. I was afraid it was a rodent. Sally lifted the woman's skirt. There lay, by the grace of God, this baby. The rest, you know."

Louise returns with a clean chamber pot half full of water. I test the temperature. Louise and Francine stay with the baby, and I practice with the aspirator. It serves two purposes. I don't remember what went through it the last time I used it. Seems like a lifetime ago. And working the valves, it gives me the feel of how much to draw and how much suction to use. I have never used it on a baby, and the difficulty of finding a doctor at this hour with more expertise makes it obvious I have no other choice than to attempt to help the child. I return to the table with my instrument and its catch basin. The baby mistakes the drawing tube for her mother's nipple and helps me create the suction I need, and bit by bit I can draw out the fluids obstructing her lungs. Almost immediately, she lets go of the tube with her lips and coughs out more thick, bloody mucus. Alice is there with a washcloth and dabs the baby's face clean. I remove the aspirator and apply the stethoscope again. Heartbeat strong. Breathing not so ragged.

"Here," I motion to Francine. "Listen."

She caresses my hands as I place the listening ends in her ears. She listens intently, and I see her recognition as I move the business end around the baby's chest and stomach.

She hands them to Alice, whose intensely furrowed countenance turns into a surprised and happy smile as she hears the heartbeat and lungs working like tiny bellows.

I finish my examination of the baby, wiping away the last vestiges of childbirth from her tiny body. I count all the digits. Her head is not misshapen from too much time in the birthing canal. Joints move freely and at correct angles. She appears healthy to my untrained eye. I will summon a colleague with more experience later this morning. A brown line on her right buttock, like a miniature question mark, refuses to disappear. A birthmark, maybe?

"She sounds much better," Alice says. "May I hold her?"

I nod. My work is done, and I sigh with relief. Francine is crying. What happened to Louise? She is nowhere about. Alice takes the baby, rewraps the swaddling blanket, stands and gently coos into the baby's ear.

My attention returns to the basket, and I lift out a scone. "What?" I stare back at their shocked expressions. "It is my payment for services rendered." I pour myself some tea and enjoy the moment. The clock rings twice. This is an excellent reason for disturbing my slumber. It warms my heart to be useful again. This is an acceptable result, but I'm afraid it is still too soon to return to my practice. I have much to learn about myself, my full self. There is much inner work I have to do. Then there is the matter of fulfilling my promise to Francine, helping her create a permanent home for New Hope. We are close to taking title of a building in Whitechapel. Then we have to gut it and transform it into her vision.

"May I?" Francine asks. She appears hesitant and unsure, not the woman I am quite fond of with her steely determination and purposeful actions on behalf of the fallen women of Whitechapel. Alice slides the baby from her shoulder to Francine's. "Gently, like you are holding an injured bird."

Tenderly, Francine sways and smiles through her tears. This is a side of her hidden from me since the day we met. There are new sides to me as well. In this moment, I am allowed a peek into her enormous heart and cannot help but feel deeper affection for her.

Louise bursts into the room. "Mrs. Summerberry says you can borrow these for as long as you need, Doctor Jekyll," she says breathlessly. She produces two baby bottles. Louise had run from her house on the opposite side of the square and back in record time.

Milk is warmed, and Alice feeds the baby as we look on.

"This changes things, Henry," Francine says to me. Her eyes meet mine, and I want to stare into them for eternity. I am unsure where this will take me, us.

"How so? I am housing eight single women, a dog and my house staff," I say. "Between us all, I am sure we can keep her healthy until a proper home is found for her."

Francine sniffs back and answers quickly, "Of course, you're right. A proper home, yes."

The constable Sally summoned last night walks up to us on Commercial Street as we begin our respective rounds. Heavyset with farmer's hands, he is stout and dressed warmly with a blue serge overcoat and coarse wool trousers of the same color. Fog shrouds the storefronts and lampposts, swallowing all shadows and muffling the clatter of carts and carriages.

"Mrs. Murphy, the do-gooder, why aren't you home sleeping in a warm bed on such a foul evening?"

"You ask me that question every time we meet, Constable Collier." He understands my mission and is one of the few members of the constabulary who doesn't make life miserable for the Whitechapel unfortunates by harassing them or demanding sexual favors.

"It is an awful mess you involved me in. The poor girl had no identification on her. We found a scrap of paper with an address on it, and we think she got turned around, lost. Did the baby survive?"

"Yes, a healthy baby girl. We are caring for her until her family can claim her or she is put up for adoption." I say without conviction. "Doctor Jekyll completed the task. Her lungs appear normal, the same for her appetite." All the women staying at Henry's house took turns feeding her, except me. After the feeding, I drifted off to sleep and dreamed about Henry and I raising a child of our own someday.

"I will make a supplemental report." Collier pencils notes onto his pad and returns them to an interior pocket. "You did well. You saved the baby. Remember that."

Sally asks, "Did they find her purse or any of her belongings when it got light out?"

"Nothing, but the inspectors think she arrived from Holland. Her shoes have that styling. We are hoping whoever sent her or was to receive her will make a missing person report."

"Were there any signs of foul play?" I ask.

Collier shakes his head. "The coroner will make the final determination as to the manner and cause of death, but we are operating under the assumption she died giving birth. We are checking the address on the scrap of paper. It might offer some clues."

I shudder at the thought of the poor girl confused, wandering alone around this part of London, where street signs are a luxury, getting robbed, experiencing labor pains, and knowing she is about to give birth. Her waxen face and pained stare of death will stay with me forever.

"Find the girl's family," Sally pleads.

Collier asks, "What if they don't want to be found? What if she was banished?"

Collier's observation pierces my heart like an arrow. He reminds me I am a woman who had a miscarriage and drank herself out of a marriage.

Thanks to Mrs. McCreary, who took me in and ministered to me, I won my battle with the bottle and took shaky steps forward. She is why I work with women who drink themselves out of marriages, jobs, and families. Like me, they may never repair those broken relationships, but they can move forward with sober dignity. There are successes. Sally's mother is coming around. I can see the pride she has in her daughter winning her battle with the devil. Some of my other ladies, like Louise, made amends and have earned their family's trust again. So, I visit this decrepit and sin-filled section of London almost nightly. My goal is to help them name their shame, regret, and guilt, and help them move onward with dignity and integrity. This mission helps me heal the ache in my heart from the loss of what could have been in my marriage and motherhood.

Sally and I visit the side streets and alleys near the saloons and gin palaces where the ladies ply their trade. We avoid the alley where we found the baby and her dead mother. The horror of the discovery was still fresh in our beings. Plenty of men are out braving the elements to find their pleasure. The number of women offering services far outnumber them, and as the morning trudges on, the entreaties become louder and more brazen, the offers more desperate for this last weekend of November. The fierce competition among the women pierces the fog.

Desperate for another drink, desperate for a final payout to afford a bed in a doss house, a few women tussle when they claim the same man. He turns away from both of them and directly into my path. In the light of the Ten Bells Pub, I recognize him. At first, I am shocked. What is he doing out here engaging with prostitutes? Then I become angry.

"Seamus Murphy, what are you doing here?" I used my loud voice to let everyone within earshot know who is standing before me. I am not one to make a scene, but when my estranged husband has women pulling on his sleeves after midnight on the seedy side of London, I give myself permission to get vocal.

He jerks his head up from surveying the slick cobblestones and stops at the sound of my voice. "Looking for you, Francine." He is dressed better than on the day we married. Gleaming boots, tall hat and coattails, he could be mistaken for a West End gentleman pursuing prurient pleasures. He removes his topper and to reveal jet black hair and piercing blue eyes. He is clean-shaven and tall, broad shouldered and heart-stoppingly handsome.

"You're a far cry from Rosemary Lane. Nary a word from you for two years, and you come to Whitechapel looking for me. You think I sell my body? You think I am a fallen woman?"

He holds the brim of his hat close to the vest, but his words are spoken quietly in our County Cork brogue. "I know what you do for these ladies of the evening. I know you have not touched a drop o' whiskey since our parting. I need to talk to you about something important." He looks at Sally, then back at me.

"Whatever you have to say to me, you can say it in front of her." Both Sally and I take up fist-on-hips positions across from him.

"It's about my sister, Rosie."

My first impulse is to ask why I would be interested in talking about the witch who convinced Seamus to throw me out on my backside following my one and only blackout. "Go on then. Out with it."

He scans the gathering bystanders. He looks at Sally and finally settles his gaze on me. "She needs your help. We need your help."

My anger cools like the mist settling on slick surfaces. For that moment, the fog lifts around us, and I see into his heart. It must be something very important to track me down on the other side of the Thames at this hour of a work night.

"Walk with us. Be mindful of your step. They don't take the same care of the streets in Whitechapel." Sally flanks Seamus on his other side, and we make our way across the street. The show is over, and the business of buyers and sellers returns as a dozen more women and men exit the pub.

"Did you know her husband, Jimmie O'Sullivan died this summer?" he asks.

"How?"

"Cargo net let loose, and all hell rained down on him."

"Rosie?"

"She couldn't leave her bed, I took her in. Only right thing to do with her being widowed and so far along with his child."

"What's this got to do with me?" I ask. She was angry with me when I miscarried before she married O'Sullivan. She assumed the drink had something to do with it. Looking back, I had no right to argue that point with her. I drank. I had a miscarriage. I drank more until I drank myself onto the street. I knew Rosie had been trying to get pregnant with O'Sullivan.

"She wants to meet with you. Tomorrow, noon at Mary McCreary's shop. It's best you hear it from her. She thinks you can do something about her…. predicament."

"And you, what do you think, Seamus?"

"She is desperate."

"And?" Our eyes meet. It's been over two years since we had talked. Some things can be said without words between husband and wife. I search his face for clues. The woman I was is not the woman standing before him this damp cold late autumn morning. I am different, and so is he. We are not the same madly in love childhood sweethearts we once were. I need to hear what he thinks.

"I wouldn't be here if I thought I was taking on a fool's errand."

4

At the sound of the approaching cab, I pull back the curtain. The legal papers Utterson prepared for New Hope can wait. After Francine presented me with a baby in distress, I dared not rest my eyes until she arrived from her nocturnal visits to Whitechapel anymore. I worry now about her more than I did when Saucy Jack crisscrossed the cobblestone streets hunting the same women she was trying to rescue. Why is that? My feelings for her have grown. She knows that for a fact, but it is her feelings for me that have captured my heart and mind. Me, Henry Jekyll, the aloof and ponderous doctor with a terrible secret. She cares about me. We've not talked about it much since that night on the docks, what with our work with our mission, a houseful of women weaning off the devil's drink, and days filled with baking the most incredible treats found this side of the English Channel.

I will remain dressed until she retires to her room next to mine. In the mirror, I spy the door that connects our sleeping quarters. The bolt operates from her side. I insisted on giving her that assurance she would be safe with me.

The horse brings the hansom to a stop in front of my

mansion on Cavendish Square. Two women alight. The red-haired beauty who sets my heart afire is first. Then, Sally hands the driver her basket before he helps her down to the curb. Francine pays him, and then Sally allows him to paw about the basket for a suitable tip. I can hear his repeated cockney 'thank-youse' from here. The voices wake Lucky, and I hear him tear through the house to the front door. His barking changes the instant Francine calls his name.

I feel relief. They bring me no more babies this dreary morn. With certainty I can say, the house will settle into much needed slumber. Francine is unstoppable in her quest, but she has youth and drive on her side. I am over twice her age and have trouble keeping up with her some days. The ladies smile knowingly when I slip off to my study before afternoon tea for my pipe and newspaper and return a few hours later with former unlit and the latter unread.

Louise Anderson greets them at the door. She is the new house matron. My butler, Poole, is older than I, ancient by some standards. He served my father before me and has always had my best interests in mind. His rooms are in the rear. He makes sure the gardener, cook and cleaners perform to his high standards. He schedules the deliveries of provisions and juggles my business appointments. The bevy of high-spirited women discovering sobriety channel their energy into baking and sewing clothes. He skirts the kitchen, pantries and sewing rooms as they shock his staid personage.

I am forever grateful to Louise; more than once she connected me to Francine when all seemed lost. My duplicity, erratic behaviour and convenient blackouts never swayed her from believing in my genuine desire to assist the woman who rescued her from the streets. Her now deceased brother, so amazed by Louise's transformation, arranged a meeting for Francine to ask me to fund her mission. As a sexton at the church I no longer attend, he knew that my unfulfilled pledge to

St. Giles would more than make Mrs. Murphy's dreams a reality. His sister is living proof of Francine's tireless belief that a black sheep lost in the dark can be found and returned to the light.

The stairway creaks as Francine makes her way upstairs. Louise and Sally remain on the ground floor with the other women. Tomorrow, I will ask Francine to bring me one of Sally's scones upon their return as an excuse to see her one more time before we retire. I can ask her about her night's work, and it will give us a chance to talk about the boring but necessary legal steps needed to take title of the future site for New Hope.

Her door from the hallway opens. Dare I dream that one evening she will instead open the door to my room and make her way to my bed? Such thoughts and arousals are more common and resilient these days against my weakening protestations. I must tell her sooner than later of these thoughts and desires. Not to find myself entwined in her naked embrace with her hair spilling down my face and chest, but to alert her to Edward Hyde's randy nature sharing my heart, mind, and loins. I find myself thinking thoughts, feeling feelings, and imagining scenes in a play which would make Shakespeare blush. Words form in my brain I would never utter, yet they are there as proof. I am changing. Is it for the better? Not sure if it is safer? I came out of the protected shell formed when Hyde shielded me from the horrors of my early childhood. Much thought has gone into this new and changing reality. I keep reminding myself; I am more capable now than as an adolescent or young man full of hubris to deal with the transformative effect of becoming one whole person. Secretly, I worry he will become dominant.

Francine's bedroom floorboards tell me of her path to her wash basin. Splashing water allows me to visualize the grime and soot released from her exquisite face. I speculate about her towel blotting the water from her brow and piercing green eyes. The eyes that arrested me on our first meeting and have kept me imprisoned since.

Those nights on the island when I awoke in a hammock beneath palm trees as a lightning storm and thunder enveloped me is nothing like the sensations coursing through my body as I consider her slowly shedding clothing before pulling on sleeping attire.

A knock on the door between our rooms causes me to leap to my feet. Dry mouthed with a headful of prurient thoughts, I chastise myself with heart-pounding dread. Can she read my mind? Is she coming to admonish me? "Yes?" I croak.

"I saw your lamp was still lit. I have brought you a present," she says.

Banishing the last of my imaginations of her unclothed loveliness, I remember my manners. "Please come in."

The bolt clicks. The doorknob turns. The door swings inward. Lamplight from her dresser casts her shadow into my space. A scent of cinnamon wafts to my nostrils. Hands in a closed prayer position beneath bare arms make me gulp. No spit to relieve my parched throat. She is wearing a plain pale blue dress with house slippers covering sockless feet. "The last one. I thought you would like it." She smiles and unclasps her hands and offers me a treat.

Dumbstruck, I receive it and nod in thanks. I am reduced to gestures. I've seen semi-conscious patients react with more emotion. Hand to mouth, I take a bite of the warm scone. Then another. I must reply to her perplexed stare. Satisfied she didn't read my mind—only Edward could do that—I regained some semblance of civility and pointed her to my chair. "Forgive my manners, Francine. The baby is well and showing no signs of its previous distress," I report.

"I know; it was the first thing I asked Louise when I came in the door."

"How did you and Sally make out this cold, foggy, wet morning?" The thought of dropping the scone and surrounding her in a warm embrace causes me to stifle a cough.

"The weather put a damper on the number of men out there. Foreign sailors with money from their last port of call, looking for companionship, did not interest any of the women, and many retreated to their lodgings as the weather worsened." She shakes her head and allows her long hair to frame her face. She stares at me and, for once, I detect this fiery Irishwoman is at a loss for words. She points to the other chair at my writing table. I sit as if commanded, and on cue, Lucky trots in from her room. He stands between us on hind legs, and a portion of my scone rewards his efforts. I take another bite and wait for this woman and dog, who are so inclined, to visit my bed chambers. We have had a few intimate talks before, and it was me who did most of the talking.

"Some of what I am about to tell you I've told to Mary McCreary and God. Only one cared." She reaches down to pet our dog. "Between Edward and you, I know all your secrets, and I am still here with you. We can do much together, Henry."

Flickering lamplight, shadows playing on the wall, a dog licking my fingers and my hand brushes against hers as it sometimes does. I wait.

"In the Pope's eyes, I am still married to Mr. Murphy. His first name is Seamus. He found me in front of the Ten Bells Pub tonight and talked to me for the first time in nearly three years."

5

Henry withdraws his hand from Lucky's furry neck, sits up straight and crosses his long legs, pulling his feet under the chair. "You never mentioned his first name to me," he says.

"Our families came to Liverpool during the blight." I stare down at Lucky. He's not judging me if licking my hand and wagging his tail is any sign. "Finding it overcrowded, they made their way here twenty-odd years ago. I was but a wee sprite. Both of our parents are dead. I was the only child to survive on my side. Seamus has a sister, Rosie; no other kin to speak of."

"I see." He examines lint on his trousers. We are exploring something new for him. My past.

I wait until he looks at my face. "There was never a question that Seamus and I would marry, but Rosie made it clear no girl was good enough for her big brother. You hear it often enough, you start to believe it. I'm sure you understand."

He nods.

Are you daft, Francine? Of course, he understands. His childhood was a nightmare. Same goes for his brother, George. I address the other party in this conversation. "Lucky, you had a rough patch too. Now look at the three of us. Anyway, somehow my husband must have learned about how I spend my nights and tracked me down."

"To reconcile?"

"No. Why would you ask me that?"

Just as quickly, he responds, leaning forward and placing both hands on his knees. "You're sober, industrious and even more beautiful because of what you have gone through. Surely, Mr. Murphy can see that."

It's my turn to register surprise as warmth spreads from my heart to my throat and finally tingles my cheeks and earlobes.

He says, "I often wished Mr. Murphy was panning for gold in California or…." Henry can't utter the unthinkable.

"No, he is alive and well, living in London, a lucky lighterman sought after by most of the shipping companies," I counter.

"I didn't mean to imply…"

"But that is what you were thinking, and I can understand why. You are not the only one seeking distance from your past. I never told you about him or why he left me."

"Certainly, you had good reason for your privacy," he said.

"As did you, Henry. Until recently, I had good reason not to trust you completely. Now that you know Seamus has contacted me, I want you to know the rest of my story."

With that said, both of our right hands return to petting our canine companion.

"After Ma died, Da drank himself to death. Whiskey was his poison, and he always had plenty of it around. He confessed to me things he was not proud of. I often wondered how the man who couldn't find honest work always had a full liquor cabinet, yet my conscience had no problem drinking from it."

Looking Henry straight in the eye, I saw no warning signs to back off. The more I told this wonderful man, the surer I was, he would understand why it is time to tell him about my past. "I would be lying to you if I said I didn't have a thirst for it, too. Gin made me sick, but a good Irish whiskey kept me warm on many a chilly night after me da died before I married Seamus. If Seamus told me an unopened bottle fell into his lighter, I didn't question him while I went to rinse out two glasses to toast our good fortune." Good times with Seamus and a wee bit of drink rushed my thoughts from behind the locked doors of my memory.

"He likes it too, but knew when to stop. Our gay life held promise. We would make a family and find a house to call our own. Money was tight, but we saved. That was one thing our parents taught us. After his ma died from consumption, it made no sense for Rosie to live with strangers, and we took her in."

"Envy is a powerful thing; look what it did to George," he said. "The arguments we had in public were just the beginning."

"I couldn't keep house. Her mother was a better cook. My coat was tired. My shoes were always scuffed. Every time we had cause for celebration, she would dampen the mood. It was so bad, Seamus and I would steal away to our bedroom to sneak a toast to our good fortune." The tightness in my throat relaxes. The weight on my chest lifts. I work hard not to take strolls down memory lane. What I have now is precious. What the stars have planned for me is wondrous. I need always to listen to my heart, but this good and righteous man deserves an explanation. I've held these secrets in for too long, and it feels right in this moment.

He smiled. At first, it confused me. Then he said, "George reminded me often how I was a heathen for abandoning the church."

We laughed lustily, with gallows humor. Lucky doesn't see us laugh together often. It is something we should practice. We. Us.

"Then I got pregnant. Where Rosie could have been a sister

to me, her attacks became more virulent. The die was cast when Seamus took a backhand to her one hot summer night after working since dawn on the stinking river. From that point on, she stopped talking to us when we were all present. She stopped talking to me altogether. I would pretend to go to the corner store for supper items and sneak back home to hear her letting loose on my Seamus. Later, I would ask him why he continued to take her guff. He said he was the only family she had. I was not considered her family in his eyes either, and as a nervous first-time mother to be, sick from the heat, and sick from God know what, I took to sneaking drinks to calm my nerves."

"At first it helped," he said. "Then as you got further along." He waited for me to continue.

"Seamus worked longer hours, something about having to provide for four mouths to feed. Rosie refused to talk to me. The neighbours knew my predicament and kept their distance. Father Callahan told me to do the Rosary. I did it until my fingers bled. Other mothers couldn't understand my pain. Looking into the faces of their gaggles of children, I could understand why. They had encountered nothing I was talking about."

Lucky rarely sits in my lap, but when he asks I let him. Henry reclines. He is a doctor and knows what I'm going to say happened next, but he has to let me tell my truth.

"Then one night, Seamus didn't come home. None of the other men who worked the docks would talk to me. They seemed in evil spirits. Rosie broke her silence long enough to say that he left us, and it was my fault. I feared the worst. Not that he left me, but that the others were waiting for Father Callahan and a constable to come by the flat and make notification my man had died and wasn't coming home. Accidents were common occurrence on the docks, and my imagination ran wild. To this day, I believe the baby sensed my distress and was overcome by it. I drank some to calm my nerves. I thought it would calm the baby, too. I drank some more. At some point, I passed out. Hours later, I woke with a start. The baby was coming. I screamed in pain. Rosie came running in, took one look at me and said, 'You're drunk,' and slammed the door. My baby boy arrived stillborn. I was alone, disoriented, with not a hand to hold or an angel to call upon. I lay there until Seamus came home. When? Well, after daylight. He had worked all night and was excited to tell me he had made triple his normal fare to unload tea from India. That is why the other men were mad at him. They didn't get to share in his bounty. He looked at me, at our dead baby, sat down on the bed, put his face in his hands and cried. All I could think was, what did I do to kill his baby?"

I took a deep breath. Henry was leaning forward, his knees nearly touching mine. He reached over and took both of my hands in his. Lucky didn't seem to mind.

"My world fell apart. I was in a fog when we buried our baby boy. I drank more. I wanted to kill myself. I couldn't leave my bed, and I stopped eating. Seamus removed all the spirits from the house. I searched everywhere. I should have taken a cleaning rag around all the surfaces I touched. Rosie was nowhere to be found. I threw on some clothes, dragged myself around the corner to where I had lived with my da and broke down the door, went to what had been his bedroom and pried up a floorboard and sure enough my best friend in the world was waiting for me."

"Francine, I am sorry." Henry moves his chair over next to mine, and he holds me in his arms and rocks me slowly. His touch is like an oasis with cool waters quenching a thirst two years in the making. Was I still longing for the arms of my husband as Henry held me?

"Three days later, I woke up from a blackout, sitting like we are now. Mary McCreary was holding me like my ma did when

I was sick as a child. She told me I had a new home, and everything was alright. To this day, I still don't know what I said to Seamus or Rosie, but it must have been bad." Lucky feels the need to stand on Henry's arm and lick away my tears.

6

My feet take me from the West End towards Mary McCreary's store. The sun rises in front of me into the blue sky, promising an unseasonably pleasant day. Its brightness chases away all clouds. Weak rays warm the air and dry out the streets. Horses pulling carts and cabs seem to have a little more bounce in their step. I am not sure why I am walking with this much vigor either. I did sleep deeply and dreamlessly after departing Henry's room. Could a good night's rest and a sunny day be enough?

Henry and I were puzzled by the cryptic way Seamus relayed Rosie's request. We didn't talk about it at breakfast with the other woman. Sally was smart to stay mum on the subject. The baby was passed from shoulder to shoulder until Alice wrestled her away from Louise. No word on who the mother was yet.

The newest arrivals to the Jekyll mansion came as a package, and I ask myself if Alice caring for the newborn of a woman who she heard die giving birth will help her stay sober. I remind myself I left Alice surrounded by other sober women who all had been called drunken whores in recent times. She awoke in a warm bed, in a beautiful house, with clean clothes, food, and delicious baked goods awaiting her. This is the mission of New Hope. Can I trust Alice to take on this added responsibility while she treads the hot coals out of hell? What happens when her body craves the devil's drink? Will the baby's needs become too much? I never planned to care for women with infants in tow.

As I get closer to the Thames, my thoughts turn to Seamus, who plies this waterway for his living. He has a brightly colored lighter, but he usually works closer to the warehouses and docks on the Southside. He delivered his message and departed quickly that morning. At first, I thought it was because he gets on the water shortly after dawn. Then I questioned how he felt walking amongst the boozy streetwalkers, making suggestive comments and come-on to him. Seamus never had to pay for it, and someone from church spying on him in Whitechapel would start the gossip flying. I can take what he said at face value. It was important he find me and give me a message. Why did Rosie want to meet with me, and why did she choose Mary McCreary's store to be the meeting spot? These remain the two questions that have occupied my thoughts since Seamus left Sally and me on the street in front of the Ten Bells Pub.

Mary's store is mid-block; it serves the Irish community and now the flood of immigrants from Europe—Poles, Hungarians and Slavs. They point, and she separates the coins and gives them exact change. Word gets around that she is an honest merchant. After money changes hands, she usually adds a treat or two with a wink and a smile. McCreary's is printed in gold leaf over the arched window above the doorway. Colorful signs advertising soaps and stomach cures fill both display windows on either side. A bell announces my entrance, and I quickly move to the side where Mary stands over her ledger on a glass counter. Her eldest, Paddy, calls out a number from atop a ladder where he is placing items on the highest shelf. Mary writes it down. The process goes on interrupted while the two finish adding the new inventory. Gabrielly serves customers quickly, with money flying into and out of the cash box below the front counter. Her other two children, the youngest, keep the floors and shelves clean and spotless. Gabby spies me first. "Ma, it's Francine paying us a visit."

I receive hugs from each. Finally, Mary steers me outside. "Too nice to stay inside, we will wait for her on the sidewalk." A breeze moves the air towards the river, and the smells of breakfast cooking and baking waft over us from neighbouring buildings; the tenants' windows are open, receiving fresh air one more time before winter hammers them closed with icy cold.

"Imagine my surprise when Seamus came round looking for you," she said. "Shoulda seen the look on his face when I told where he could find you."

"Did he say want he wanted?" I asked.

She shook her head. "Only that he wanted to set up a meeting with you and Rosie O'Sullivan."

"I knew she was married to O'Sullivan from talking to you," I say.

"Ay, but there's something I didn't mention to you," Mary says.

"What's that?"

"It's better if it comes from her mouth," my saviour says.

"Now you have me wondering, Mary," I say. "First Seamus and now you."

"You can ask her yourself. The girl's early, and by the looks of her, something terrible has happened again."

Again? I think before spinning around. Black coat and skirt, white blouse, no pearls, and a black hat usually worn to a funeral is my first impression of the tall, thin, black-haired woman with the pasty complexion. Below the brim are red, teary eyes and a mouth about to say something urgent.

"Well, I must be getting back to my bookkeeping, now that youse have met. Tell Seamus I was present."

"No, stay, Mary. I want you to hear this. All of this. I need you both to hear this." Rosie's voice was hoarse with emotion. How long has she been in this state?

"What's wrong?" I ask. Forget that she made my life miserable and made my marriage feel like Seamus and I were in a rowboat during a raging storm. Spending time on these very streets with women at their wit's end has given me some emotional distance while still being able to connect.

"How can I ask you to forgive me for all the terrible things I did to you? How can I ask your forgiveness when I never considered doing so until I had an awful need?" She counts on her fingers. "I was selfish when I didn't want you to marry Seamus. I thought I needed my older brother more than you needed a husband. I was envious of you that you married a handsome man. I saw how other men looked at you Francine, you could have had your choice, but you took my only brother, my only family. The terrible things I did and said after you took me in when Ma died. Was I grateful for the roof over my head, the food you cooked, the clothes you washed, sowed and mended? No, I was a shrill shrew, selfish and sullen. I never had a pleasant word. I can't remember ever saying one nice thing."

"That's true. I remember you not keeping your thoughts to yourself," Mary says. "You even questioned who the father was when Francine was with child."

I look back and forth between them. The Irish can keep secrets.

Rosie nods. "That is true. I could have been like a sister to you in your time of need, but I acted like a jealous lover, saying terrible things that were not true, spreading rumors, making sure the neighbours would think you were a sleep-around while Seamus was working."

She looked at her shoes. Rosie tried some words in her mouth, her shoulders heaved, her eyes spoke of anguish now realized.

Mary says, "You realize from your own hurt how much you hurt her, tell her."

Rosie looks fearfully at Mary.

"It takes courage to admit your failings, Rosie," Mary says. "Tell her."

"Telling you Seamus left you on the night you lost the baby was unforgivable, even if you could find it in your heart to forgive me for any of my transgressions, then leaving you alone when you delivered in the morning should slam the door shut in my face forever. I would understand. I was mean, spiteful, angry, jealous and, until recently, a woman who could look in the mirror and believe her actions were justified and you were deserving of my wrath."

"But here she still stands, listening to you admit your failings. Does that tell you something about Francine?" Mary says. "So tell her what changed."

"I married O'Sullivan and wore white that day. I started showing about a month later. His kin stayed clear of me. They knew about the poison I spewed about you and towards you. They knew what I was capable of. He and I were alone, and I understood what I had done to you. Then one day I was feeling poorly and didn't go to work at the mill. I heard a knock at the door. It was a constable and Father Callahan. My world fell to pieces."

"Oh, Rosie." I reached for her and took her in my arms. She was pregnant and became a widow. That was one of my greatest fears. Seamus would not return from the river. I would be alone with nobody to help me raise our child. I am not sure how I feel about all the things she said and did to me, but I know how to show compassion to a woman who loses her man forever.

Mary McCreary knew about the death, this much I am sure. Why didn't she tell me? I get the answer to the question immediately.

Rosie pulls out of my embrace and stands with Mary and I in a perfect triangle. "After I buried my husband, his family says they don't believe he was the father of my child, that I only duped him into marrying me cuz I was pregnant. They told me they wanted nothing to do with me. They said that you were not a sleep-around, but it was me who had round heels."

"You had no place to go," Mary says.

The Irish can be a spiteful bunch, I know.

"Seamus took me back but said that I would have to make other arrangements as soon as I could get back on my feet after James was born."

"How old is James?" I ask.

"Fifteen weeks. He looks just like O'Sullivan, just so you know."

Suddenly wary, Mary asks, "Who's watching him?"

Rosie cries.

"What happened to the baby?" Mary asks.

"I should have come to you months ago, Mary. I knew what you did for Francine. I was too proud and too stupid."

"Where's the baby, woman?" Mary demands.

"I can't do anything right. I stood between you and Seamus. I put up a wall around O'Sullivan and me. I ruined any chances for a family. You could have helped me, Mary and I was too full of shame for all that I did to ask you...."

Mary's slap across Rosie's right cheek was sharp and startling. "Where is the child?"

Rosie screams, "I don't know. I don't know. James has been kidnapped. He has been sold. He is dead. He is missing. He could be on a boat to America. I don't know. You have to believe me." Rosie's body wracks in convulsions. Mary holds her tightly.

I go into the store. "Gabby, fetch me some water." I peer out the windows. A strolling couple across the street have stopped to stare. A drover looks over at Mary and Rosie with his reins in mid-command. The store is empty. I open the door and call to Mary. "Bring her inside." I hold the door for them as Gabby brings the water. The last customer edges past us. Paddy and Gabby retreat to the storeroom.

"From the beginning," I say.

Rosie gulps the water and then takes smaller swallows and mouths in a deep breath and then another and another until she stills. She closes her eyes, and we each take a hand she offers. "O'Sullivan's people would have nothing to do with me or the baby. I've no friends to speak of. Seamus told me I had to leave. That's when I decided to go to America. Start over. Clean slate. A lady runs a house here for babies. She would care for James until I could return to him. I scraped together most of the money, eight pounds. I left him in her care."

"When," Mary prodded gently, but with all urgency.

"Three days ago. I am supposed to set sail tomorrow."

"I returned with the remaining two pounds the next day. The lady acted surprised to see me. I might be a lot of things, but I am not a cheat. I asked to see James one last time, and when she didn't come back right away, I knew something was wrong. She said she had looked all over the house and questioned her staff. She said James was missing. I went back the next day. Same thing. Seamus told me to report James missing to the police. I did. That's when he said I should talk to you and Francine."

"How long was this lady to care for your baby?" I ask.

"A year."

"And if you didn't come back from America?" Mary asks.

"There are plenty of wealthy couples looking for a beautiful, healthy baby boy, and she would arrange an adoption. I signed papers making it legal, but I told her I would come back as soon as I was able for my boy, I promised her." Rosie scanned our faces.

Mary nodded.

Rosie drank more of the cup.

I saw Mary's frown matching mine. She didn't believe Rosie about that last part either.

"Doctor Jekyll, I met your associate, Mr. Hyde, in Whitechapel not too long ago. He put a blade to my throat and had some interesting things to tell me before he used my own irons on me."

Why am I not surprised Inspector Newcomen of Scotland Yard intercepts me on my way to Utterson's offices to complete paperwork for New Hope. Utterson has been my attorney and closest confidant for many years. I am to meet Francine there after her business with Rosie O'Sullivan and Mary McCreary concludes. I motion to the driver of the carriage to wait. A good tip is guaranteed when I rub my finger against my thumb.

"A man matching Hyde's description was seen running from the scene of the Ripper's third victim to date. His arm was bleeding profusely."

That same arm tingles where Jack's blade sliced my arm from wrist to elbow. All of Edward's memories fill my head now, and the dark courtyard comes back to me.

"A short while later, I spotted Hyde entering a warehouse near Francine Murphy's flat and you exiting the only door from that empty location."

I respond curtly, "And when you searched my surgery for evidence of the Ripper's nasty business, you left empty-handed. You were warned by my solicitor, any further questions would be directed to him, goo...."

Before I could dismiss him, Newcomen continued unfazed. "After Hyde brutally murdered Sir Danvers Carew, he continued to be spotted around the West End and Soho. He disappeared for the entire time you were away in the West Indies and was only spotted again upon your return, fleeing the scene of another murder and weeks later made a point of admitting to me and a constable his reasons for murdering Carew." Newcomen pointed to a thin red line where his throat and his jowl converge. I knew this bully with a badge would not let that assault pass.

I step onto the carriage step-up and reach for the handhold when he pulls me back down to the gutter. "I have no questions for you, Doctor Jekyll. The next time I see you, I will arrest you for being his accomplice." His bulk presses me up against the right rear wheel, the wooden spokes moving back and forth across my spine as the horse senses danger. The driver shifts uncomfortably on his perch, the buggy whip impotent in his hands. Might he lend it to me if I asked politely?

Normally, I would take this abuse from Newcomen, but I am a new man, emboldened and no longer afraid of his threats. It is impossible for him to find Hyde, and I have endured worse. He doesn't need to know it was I who suffered at the hands of Carew and my insane mother's other twisted paramours. Hyde has returned those memories to me, both in my mind and in my body. "I have a question for you, Inspector Newcomen." He relaxes his grip on my lapels but continues to glare into my face. "If you are so hell bent on finding the killer of Carew. This would be even more obvious to Hyde, and he knew only you and you alone stood between his freedom and the gallows. Why didn't he shove that blade into your throat when he had the chance?"

8

Rosie's apologies peter out as she pleads one more time for Mary and me to help her.

Mary replies for both of us. "We can find out more about the people running the operation than the police, what with them being preoccupied with the Ripper. Who knows when he will strike next? The entire world's attention is on Whitechapel and Scotland Yard. We might have more luck. Stop by the store before you set sail."

"I promise," she says. Hugs are offered. It's the first time I can remember my sister-in-law doing so. She leaves us on the sidewalk.

Mary waits until Rosie turns the corner before speaking "Bollocks. Who does she think she is, coming here and acting contrite? I admire you, Francine, for hearing her out."

"I did it for Seamus because he asked." At no time did Rosie say she was cancelling her trip to America, and she just confirmed our suspicions. She expects us to find Baby James for her. I stop to gather my feelings, heaving like a raft in a tempest. I am inclined to think the baby would be better off without her. Selfish, self-absorbed and manipulative are words I could use to describe my sister-in-law. Smart is another word that pops into my mind. She has no family to care for her child. Her in-laws and Seamus won't take her in. America beckons her with a fresh start. A year from now, the baby would have been placed with a family. She would be just a good-riddance memory to those left behind. I shake my head. "Say what you will about that performance, and you wouldn't be wrong, Mary McCreary, but she is still a young widow, and her baby is missing or worse."

"And she has no one to help her," Mary says. We hug genuinely. "You're a good woman, Francine," she says.

I will never tire of Mary McCreary saying that. She knows my sordid past. "Have your oldest come by with what you find out. I will send him back with my reply," I say. "Paddy has been to the house on Cavendish Square before and knows the shortcuts."

I have no trouble hailing a cab. I wave goodbye as I pass. Mary will help her because I am offering to do so. Mary gave me permission to tell Rosie to piss off, but if I can find it in my heart to help her, so can Mary. Are my intentions as honorable as Mary's? Am I doing this for Rosie, or am I helping Rosie, hoping to return to the good graces of Seamus? My thoughts return to my husband as I imagine conversations about Rosie's plight as a bridge to conversations between us. Dare I consider that a possibility? He certainly knows I am a different woman from the one he banished from our home. Am I doing this to prove to him I am worthy of his love and affection? Are my motives as pure as Mary's? Would I do this for any other woman in Whitechapel with whom I was acquainted? The answer is yes. I would. How far and to what extent? I don't really know.

"We're here." The driver says. I paid no attention to the ride on this pleasant first day of December. I couldn't describe a single person, food cart or ship passing by on the Thames.

A cab pulls in behind us. "I will take care of her fare," Henry says. He smiles at me as he pays his fare and walks towards my driver. I quickly banish thoughts of Seamus from my mind. Will Henry notice my guilty expression?

He helps me down from the carriage and holds my hand until both drivers pull away. "I just had a less than pleasant conversation with a policeman."

"Newcomen?" I ask.

"Yes, how did you know?"

"He is still looking for Hyde. Edward told me that night on the dock he had met his adversary while searching for me. It would only be a matter of time before the profane inspector paid you a visit," I say.

"And Whitechapel is still crawling with police scouring the streets and alleyways for the Ripper," he replies. We both know the truth of what happened that night.

"And that's a bad thing?"

He gives me a puzzled look.

"The constables are treating the women they encounter as potential witnesses or would-be victims. The women are being more careful, walking in pairs and being more selective in their choices. Fearing Jack may strike any night has been a powerful incentive to rethink their choice of profession. This helps me persuade them to consider New Hope as their only refuge."

"Excellent reasoning, Mrs. Murphy."

"And what about the brutish Newcomen?"

Henry shakes his head. "He is so close to the truth. I am reminded of what a doctor named Doyle said at a recent medical symposium I attended."

"Pray tell," I say.

"When you have eliminated the impossible, whatever remains, however improbable, must be the truth," Henry quotes.

"Smart doctor," I say with a hint of a smile.

"I will explain more when we finish our business with Utter-son. I must tell him about Newcomen's threats."

I nod. "I have much to discuss with both you and Utterson about my meeting with Rosie O'Sullivan."

Together, we mount the stairs, and Henry leads me to his friend's office. The waiting room comprises two black leather upholstered chairs and a cherry wood table on plush carpets. The door to the office opens. Utterson is remarkably well-maintained for a man of advanced years. He wears his silver hair like a lion's mane. Summers in France give him a healthy complexion year round. Shorter than Henry, with a trim, agile grace, he greets us with a warm smile.

"I think I have found a workaround for the building's title," he said.

The building in question is an abandoned factory in the heart of Whitechapel. The rear two stories would act as the dormitory with floor to ceiling windows. The third floor would be converted to bedrooms. The southern exposure overlooks a courtyard. We plan to convert it into gardens and grottos. The main factory floor holds exciting promise for the bakery. The front entrance will include a marquee, New Hope Mission.

He continues, "A holding company purchases the property. The main shareholders in the company are Jekyll Enterprises and F. Murphy and Associates, a limited company. Henry, you will gift Francine her share in the limited company."

I smile and nod. All of this legalistic workaround just to allow a woman to be a stakeholder in her own future. I understand his need to explain it to us. He is quite happy with his ingenious plan. Utterson blathers on about the intricate workings of how it is to be accomplished. My thoughts drift back to the baby we found in the alley, Alice's heroic actions and the happiness the baby brings to the rescues of New Hope. Will we find space in the new building to house more children rescued from the streets of Whitechapel? My thoughts turn to Constable Collier about the address the unfortunate girl was trying to find that foggy night. What about contacting Inspector Abberline for a favor? Can he spare a few minutes away from the Ripper investigation to look for a missing child?

"...Henry has made provisions in his will." Utterson's words snap me back to the present.

"I'm sorry, can you repeat the last part? I was just marveling at the fine research you have done to make New Hope a reality," I say.

"Of course, Mrs. Murphy. In the event of Henry's untimely demise, he has created a trust to keep New Hope's building and operational costs afloat in perpetuity. A rolling average of four percent of Jekyll Enterprises is set aside for this purpose."

"Henry!" I instinctively reach for his hand.

"The future of New Hope is assured," he says. "You are young and full of great ideas. You have shown time and time again your commitment to your mission. But let's not dwell on my passing; let's talk about what we can do now." He hasn't let go of my hand, and his eyes meet mine. He holds no secrets. His intentions are obvious.

How can I not love this man? He is providing not only for the mission, but for me in my old age.

"We will have the contracts drawn up as soon as you decide how you want to proceed," Utterson says.

Henry says, "I am ready to proceed. Francine?"

Both men stare at me. I have one simple question. "Should something happen to me, what would happen to New Hope? How would the mission go forward?"

"A succession plan, yes, good point, Mrs. Murphy. Have you given it any thought?" Utterson asks.

It doesn't take me more than a moment, without hesitation, I say, "Mary McCreary and Louise Anderson could take over, but I would want their permission before speaking for them."

"Of course," Utterson replies.

Henry's hand retreats from his clasp with mine to his lap. "I never thought of that possibility."

His answer tells me a great deal. In the mansion's quiet tonight, I will bring him another treat and we will talk about that possibility. Sensing an uneasy shift at the moment, I say to Utterson, "We have other matters which require your attention."

He reaches for his legal pad, turns to a fresh page with pencil in hand. "How can I be of service?"

9

"Newcomen braced me this morning on the street in front of my home. He is obsessed with finding Hyde and thinks I am the key to unlocking the mystery of his whereabouts. He's making noise about Hyde being the Ripper, saying that a man meeting his description fled the scene of the first of two murders the Ripper committed in one night," Henry says.

Utterson grasps the enormity of the situation. "If I recall, witnesses say the fleeing man was bleeding profusely with a wound to his arm. How then does that man approach another woman and butcher her?

"Logic doesn't seem to matter to Newcomen?" Henry replies.

I recall that early morning vividly. Henry came to my flat that night to check on our dog and to accompany me on my rounds, but he fell ill. I went on without him and in due course learned about the Ripper's most horrible night of terror. He took two lives in adjoining neighborhoods in a brief period. I returned home to find Henry in my bed, stinking drunk with fresh stitches in his arm from his wrist to his elbow. He told me he had no memory of the events of the morning. I didn't believe him and threw him out of my flat as soon as he could stand up. Over time, I learned more about that morning and Hyde's involvement.

"Newcomen has more faults than his single-minded pursuit of Hyde. He is a political animal and is looking to curry favor with the well-to-do and the politicians. If he can tie Carew's killer into the investigation of Jack the Ripper, he will not bother with those pesky things called facts and evidence, I am afraid," Utterson says.

"Can we hope the Ripper is finished with his nasty business and Hyde no longer shows his face in town?" I say.

"That would be helpful, but I don't expect that maniac to stop his spree. I fear he likes it too much, Mrs. Murphy." Utterson replies.

"Then what about Newcomen?" Henry asks.

"Any case against you will unravel the minute he arrests you."

"Planting evidence?"

Utterson says, "The evidence against Hyde in the Carew killing is straightforward. Tying you into any of the Ripper murders would require evidence Newcomen has withheld from the inquests. That is very dangerous for him at this late date. He would need to be on the scene of a fresh killing to snatch evidence before it is catalogued."

I nod while Henry inspects his shoes, and then he looks over to me and abruptly changes the topic. "Tell us about Rosie O'Sullivan."

I am prepared for this hand-off, but I didn't expect it so suddenly. "She is the sister of my estranged husband, Seamus." I find it best to distance myself from him while maintaining the decorum of our blessed union. She married a man named O'Sullivan this year and became immediately pregnant. O'Sullivan died in an accident on the docks, and his family would have nothing to do with either Rosie or the baby boy. Seamus gave her room and board until now. She decided to make a new life in America and is to set sail tomorrow. She made arrangements with a woman to care for the infant. She gave the baby over to the woman several days ago and found out the baby went missing the next day. Yesterday, she notified the police. She came to me and Mary McCreary, the woman who helped me turn my life around, this morning and asked for us to help find the baby."

"Missing? How does an infant go missing? It's not like they can fly on the wings of angels?" Henry states the obvious.

"And she is still planning to set sail tomorrow?" Utterson asks.

"Yes." My words hung in the air. I didn't have to wonder what both men were thinking. "She said she planned to return within a year's time; otherwise, the contract allowed the woman to put the baby up for adoption."

"Do you believe her?" Utterson asks.

"About her returning or the contract?" I needed a few seconds to consider how I wanted to portray this woman to them. Here I work with women who sell their bodies for gin and am very close to providing a working solution for some of these unfortunates in Whitechapel. Yet I am concerned about what they would collectively think of Rosie. Why would I be protective of her? Do Rosie's actions give a man yet another reason to think less of a woman in this society?

"Her returning," the barrister clarifies.

"If I owned a horse, I would fall off of it if she returned to claim her baby boy."

"Missing?" Henry tries the word on his tongue.

"Rosie said the woman was surprised when Rosie returned with the rest of the money owed."

"Surprised that Rosie returned with the money or that Rosie wanted to see the baby again?" Utterson asks.

"Or surprised when the baby couldn't be produced?" Henry asks.

"Mortified, I would imagine," I say.

"Why do you say that?" Utterson asks.

"She went to look for the baby, and the baby could not be found," I say.

Henry answers differently. "Mortified because the woman took the money, never expecting to see the girl again, and adopted out the infant to a nice wealthy family. She does it that day and has no expenses and a huge profit."

Utterson tidies the paperwork on his desk. He clears a space for his elbows and leans forward. "Mortified for a more sinister reason. This was a healthy baby, I take it."

"Several months old. Rosie didn't say the baby was sickly. She would have said something," I say. My sister-in-law would have been sure to speak of her motherly skills in nursing a sick child, not realizing how those boasts would pierce my heart like daggers as I failed to bring a healthy child into this world.

"Sadly, we cannot rule out that this missing child is dead."

"What?" Henry and I exclaim.

"There are more unwanted children than families who want to adopt. That this woman could use the full year to arrange for an adoption is noble but not practical. How much did Mrs. O'Sullivan give her?"

"Ten pounds."

"A goodly sum of money, but is that enough to feed, clothe, shelter and care for an infant for a full year?"

"No," I agree. I know what it costs to do that for adults for a month. I should have done my sums with Mary McCreary. I think we were too shocked by Rosie giving the baby up and then finding the baby missing to cipher that out.

"House mothers taking infants in for care and adoption range from the best care for the baby to the worst. In 1870, a woman was hanged for killing a child left in her care. She was suspected of killing eighteen more."

"I seem to recall that. It is rare for the Crown to hang a woman," Henry says.

"I was young and moving down from Liverpool," I confess. This woman makes Jack the Ripper look like an also-ran. How we devalue our children or value the grotesque manner of the Ripper's killings speaks volumes both ways.

Utterson stands and moves to the window behind his desk. He peers out onto the busy high street. "Others would simply take in the children, pocket the money and leave the children on doorsteps of farmhouses in the country. With more supply than demand, they became ruthless in pocketing the upfront money and abandoning the children. Children who are older find themselves in workhouses or sent overseas as indentured servants."

"It's truly a miracle," I say.

Judging by their puzzled expressions, both men had no clue what I am going to say next. "The baby Alice saved. What would have happened to her if we weren't there?"

Henry fills Utterson in. "Francine was on her rounds with a new woman, Sally, when they encountered Alice on the street. They heard a woman cry out from down an alleyway and went to investigate."

"The girl died giving birth, and Alice unwrapped the cord from around the baby's neck and gave it the breath of life. The baby is doing well, and all the women in Henry's home take turns caring for her," I say.

Henry adds, "The young girl didn't have a coin to her name, and no name on any of her belongings. Why she was in the alley and what was she doing at that hour remains a mystery."

"The local constable thinks she was going to an address written on piece of paper, got lost and that's when the baby came into this world," I say.

"Terrible shame," Utterson says.

We nod. Having subsistence funds or lack thereof seems to play as much into the survival of people in Whitechapel as any other factors, and that included the most defenseless—young women and children.

10

Francine and I walk the well-maintained streets from Utterson's offices towards our home. I still delight in calling it our home. Yes, it also includes a new baby, a dog and a baker's dozen of women making wonderfully delicious baked goods, but I can dream about it being our home alone someday. She knows my feelings on the subject, and I see glimpses of her feelings towards me. She can trust me now. What a relief. I do not need to keep secrets from her any longer. "Are you happy with the way the contracts are coming along?" I ask.

"I am happy you are happy with Utterson's ingenuity. The business of Baby James is occupying my thoughts at the moment. New Hope is my mission. It is everything I wanted after Mary McCreary picked me up from the gutter, and yet I can't help but think about the baby."

"Why? You as much said that your sister-in-law came back to make her last goodbye. She was letting go of her own flesh and blood. She treated you horribly. You owe her nothing, but I understand why you are offering to help her."

She tugs my arm the way a driver pulls on the reins of a

horse. "The women I save had been making bad choices until alcohol started making depraved choices for them. I accept them where they are and help them leave that past behind. But an innocent child brought into this world by a horrible woman doesn't make that child any less important."

"The same goes for the baby we are caring for," I say.

She takes both of my hands in hers with downcast eyes. "Part of me wants us to receive word, the baby will be reunited with the girl's kin, and part me wants to keep the baby for us." Her beautiful green eyes look into mine and my heart. "There, I said it aloud, Doctor Jekyll, our baby."

"We will have to give her a name. Lucky is already taken." I smile.

"Lucy," she says.

"Lucky and Lucy," I say.

"Lucy Murphy," she says.

"Hmmm, I was thinking Lucy Jekyll." Hyde would be proud of me making an oblique proposal of marriage now. The old Henry Jekyll would have waited until he had more time to make sure he was making a wonderful decision.

She drops my hands, and a cloud of uncertainty passes over her face. She quickly regains a smile.

"Maybe just Lucy for now," I say, saving face for both of us.

"Lucy," she says. "Lucy," she says with finality.

We walk the next block in silence. At the corner, I hail a cab.

"What are you doing?" she says. "I can see your front entrance from here."

"You will need to give the cabbie the address Rosie gave you if we are to find Baby James."

———

HENRY PAYS THE MAN, who thanks him profusely for the tip. I stare at the building. Red brick. Free standing on a corner lot. A vegetable and flower garden in the rear. It's too late in the season to grow anything but weeds.

"Talk to me," he says from over my shoulder

"What's that?" I ask.

"I was asking the building to tell me all of its secrets," he replies.

We both stare. The clip-clopping of horse hooves fade away; ravens call back and forth in the distance. A boat whistle toots long and then short from the direction of the Thames. This is a forgotten and God-forsaken corner of Whitechapel. No wonder the poor girl got lost. It took a trained professional to bring us here.

Henry says, "Bad things happen here." There is something otherworldly in his trance.

"Is there an evil presence?" After watching the transformation from Mr. Hyde into Doctor Jekyll, I don't question his observations

"Yes, I am feeling a sensation of horror. Unspeakable things go on in there."

One side of the massive front door swings outward. From the interior, I hear a child-like voice repeating a nursery rhyme. I spot a waif, barefoot, wearing a tired beige knee-length housedress, stringy-brown shoulder-length hair in dire need of combing, fluttering hands, this hand to mouth, she twirls, that hand to mouth. She spots us on the street. "Visitors," she calls back into the buildings. "Visitors coming to get a baby. Visitors coming to get a baby. Coming to get a baby." I expect to see an adult greet but out walks Constable Collier and the door quickly shuts behind him. The girl's babbling ceases.

He shakes his head at us. "Half-wit," he mutters as he descends the marble steps.

He recognizes me. "How did you know this was the address the dead girl was trying to find?"

"I didn't. I thought you were here about the missing baby."

"Missing baby? What missing baby?" he knits his brow in confusion. He looks at me and an equally confused Henry.

I introduce them. "Constable Collier, this is Doctor Henry Jekyll. He is a benefactor to my mission."

The men tip caps.

"The lady of the house, Mrs. Burrough, does not know why the dead girl was coming to this address. She wasn't expecting any girls about to give birth," he says.

"Does she meet with expectant girls?" Henry asks.

"Rarely. She tells them to come back after they deliver a healthy baby. No sense making plans if the baby doesn't survive the first week or is deformed. What's this about a missing baby?"

It is my turn to speak. "My sister-in-law planned for Mrs. Burroughs to care for her baby boy until she could return within the year from America. Rosie came back the next day to complete paying the amount due and found out her baby was missing. Rosie came back the day thereafter and reported it to the police."

"Missing you say, how does a baby go missing? What's Rosie's full name?"

"Rosie O'Sullivan, 8 Rosemary Lane."

"This place is not on my beat. I came here today as a follow-up from the first time I came here to check the address in the girl's pocket. I can ask the men on this beat about the missing baby."

"Much appreciated," Henry says.

"Strange to see you in the daylight, Mrs. Murphy."

"You too, Constable Collier. Doing this on your own time, are you?"

"Made little sense for anybody else to do it, since it was me Sally grabbed by the collar."

"Anybody asking about the whereabouts of the dead girl?" Henry asks.

Collier shakes his head.

"Make a sketch or create a photograph?" Henry asks.

"The coroner didn't think it was necessary."

"Why's that?" I ask.

"Her clothes and shoes makes him think she was Dutch. Nobody in London to show it to."

"That's a shame," Henry says. "If I had a sketch or a photograph, I could get a man to go to the docks and interview the sailors on the passenger ships and ferries from Amsterdam, Antwerp, and Calais."

"She was pretty and very pregnant, might have needed help to get on board," I said.

Collier scratched the stubble on his right cheek with the back of his left hand. "I'll see if I can get permission to get two sketches done. One for the station and one…"

"For us," I say.

"And if your man finds a name on the manifest?"

"You will be the first to know, Collier," Henry says.

"Very well, must get home for some sleep. I am on duty again tonight. Extra shifts as long as the Ripper is about," he said.

"What can you tell us about Mrs. Burrough?" I ask.

"Widow, house left to her. She's trying to keep it from falling down around her ears by taking in babies. Only saw the parlor. Don't know where the brats are hiding."

"What's she like?" I ask.

"Life has dealt her a bad hand; she acts like she deserves more. Dead husband, half-wit daughter. Doesn't take too kindly to being asked questions."

"That gives me an idea," I say. "What is your first name?"

"Clarence. Why?"

"Nice to know you, Constable Clarence Colliers." I give the puzzled policeman a hug.

"Henry, shake his hand to show the woman peering through the drapes we are old friends."

Collier goes along with the ruse, not sure of knowing why. We all smile and wave goodbye as I quickly whisper into Henry's ear.

11

I think of all the colleagues at my gentleman's club and settle on Blackwell. "My friend Clarence tells me your name is Burrough. Is your husband any relation to the Wrexham Burroughs?" A Welsh mining town where Jekyll Import and Exports has interests. "This is my wife, Caroline. I am Edward Blackwell. We are here to find a suitable heir to the throne. Isn't that right, dear?" Affecting an imperious tone is easy, as I have observed my acquaintances many times talk to waiters and staff from the end of their upturned noses.

Francine nods shyly.

"And how do you know the pesky policeman?" Burrough's auburn hair is drawn back in a severe bun. I guess her age to be between Francine and me. She stands so straight you would think she had a yardstick attaching the corset from her neck to her tailbone. Hers was a robin's egg pastel dress without a horizontal waist seam, instead molded to the body by vertical seams and tucks, creating a body-hugging silhouette. I imagine a blue celery stalk. No amount of face cream can erase years of worry lines and bitterness.

"Clarence Colliers sits on vestry with me at Trinity Paddington," the lie rolls easily off my tongue.

"No, my deceased husband, Drayton, was a haberdasher in Mayfair."

I move on without offering my condolences. "Sad business Clarence is dealing with. A dead girl with no identification on her but a slip of paper directing her to this address." I left the statement hanging in the air, begging a response.

It goes unanswered. "You would like to adopt a boy, Mr. Blackwell?"

"Yes, we would." There is no hint of an Irish lilt in Francine's reply.

"You could go home with a girl, two girls within a fortnight."

Francine looks at me. How close to her heart is this role-play. We haven't moved a step out of the foyer.

The waif peers at us from behind the solid oak bannisters to the threadbare carpeted stairway. I hear her repeat twice, "Two girls in a fortnight, two girls in a fortnight."

"Yes, my family demands an heir to the Blackwell estate." I give a tired sigh. "Eddie, stop running off Africa on safari, they said." I shake my head. "Find a nice girl, they said." I reach for Francine/Caroline's hands. "And so I have." I turn to our host and say softly, "And make lots of babies, they said."

Francine settles her face on my chest. An unexpected public closeness between husband and wife. We've not been this close since that morning on the docks. I clench her to me. My feelings are not an act.

Over the top of her head, I say, "We must have a boy, but who knows what the good Lord will bring." It does not bother me a whit that my first child may be a girl, with the name of Lucy, who will be loved by her father and mother and protected by the dog, Lucky.

My brother George was to marry and produce the continuation of the Jekyll lineage. As long as I was jousting with Edward

Hyde, the thought of bringing children into this world was preposterous. To the men at the club, the vestry at St Giles and to Utterson, George is away in Turkey on urgent business.

We end our embrace, and I spy tears on Francine's cheeks. She rubs them against my topcoat and turns to face Mrs. Burroughs. "May we see how you care for the children?" My bride of ten minutes asks. We hurriedly planned this ruse upon bidding adieu to our new friend, Collier. But her tears are not fake. She miscarried her first child and doesn't know if she will carry another to term.

Burroughs interrupts our contrivance of marital affection. "The boys are kept on the second floor; the girls on the third floor. My rooms are on the top floor. I have nurse-maids for each floor working twelve-hour shifts. I fetch a wet nurse from the neighborhood when a boy.....child doesn't take to the bottle. First, come into my office so we can talk about the financial arrangements."

Francine moves in that direction, and I gently pull her back. "The tour first, Mrs. Burrough. I want to know how well you care for the future, Mr. Blackwell, before I make a deposit."

I watch her eyebrows rise with the word deposit. "In all due time, there is a process I follow." She extends her arm with an open-palmed hand towards the parlor.

"I must insist, Mrs. Burroughs, on a tour first." I say. Rosie had told Francine that Baby James has a birthmark behind the left ear, if we were so incredibly fortunate to spot him today? What would we do? Whisk him out the door to the nearest police station and wait for Rosie and another family member to identity the baby as an O'Sullivan?

"You say you are friends with the constable?"

"Come Sunday to the early service, half-seven, I will escort you to his pew myself. We have a lovely gathering in the under-croft afterwards between services." I smile. I am enjoying myself in this delicious cat-and-mouse game.

A sour expression crosses her face. I doubt her shadow has crossed a narthex since the day she buried Mr. Burroughs. I know her genuine interest is in how we are acquainted. A policeman takes his leave, and a nosy couple confers with him before arriving unannounced.

"Please," Francine asks.

Fifteen boys, four to a room with the last room by the servant's stairwell holding only three and an unmade crib. Baby James's? I wonder. They appear well nourished, the young, cheerful nursemaid talking and cooing to the boy she was changing. You'd expect the smell of urine and soiled diapers. She called out, "Felicity."

On command, the waif appeared and scooped up a pile wrapped in a sheet. "To the laundry we will go, to the laundry we will go, hi-ho the Derry-o, to the laundry we will go" and off she scampers between her mother and Francine down the back stairs, bare feet pounding on the wooden treads.

Each crib had a future date written and a star next to it. I point and ask the nursemaid about the date for the unmade crib as it is a year from tomorrow and there is no star.

That is the date the mother reclaims her child, or the baby is adopted out. The star shows the baby has new parents who paid a deposit for the adoption. Baby James didn't have a loving family willing or desperate enough to wait an entire year. Or would they have to? A bidding war?

We take those back stairs to the third floor. Darker rooms, more crowded. Five or six girls in the room. Quieter. More odorous. The nursemaid shares a similar dour expression as Mrs. Burrough. Her movements are deliberate, precise and lack any of the cheerfulness shown the boys. None of the girls are active; they all seem to sleep deeply. Their wrappings and clothing have felt the washboards too many times. She turns to Francine and says, "I do what I can to make them peaceful." The girl who is being changed doesn't wake from her slumber. I do not see any signs of bedsores on the baby. Her buttocks are healthy, but pale pink.

All the cribs have dates, and none have stars. I wonder what happens to the girls whose care period expires without finding parents?

We return to the main stairwell, which separates the house equally in half, and descend. Mrs. Burrough leads us to the parlor, which serves as her office. A roll-top desk set diagonally in one corner. Tired brown and black leather couches along the load-bearing walls, a fireplace and mantle on the center wall. Cheery gold-colored drapes let in sunlight. I stop. She turns.

I hand her Utterson's card. "This is my solicitor. He will make any financial arrangements when you come into possession of a healthy boy."

She takes the card. "There is a waiting list for boys given up immediately for adoption."

"The Blackwells don't wait in line. We have two more houses to visit before dinner. I hope to see you on Sunday." Both our smiles are fixed in place as I guide an unusually compliant Francine to the door and out into the mid-afternoon sunshine.

"I have to wash my hands and face. I feel dirty," she says between gritted teeth.

"That is one of the better ones, I imagine, Caroline, my love."

An elbow in my ribs lets me know the acting is over.

12

I stay in the carriage while Henry darts into Utterson's offices. I can't wait to return home to change my clothes and wash my face and hands. I felt the horror there, as did Henry. He told me about hearing Hyde screaming at him not to go in.

In my work in Whitechapel. I have had women throw up on me, lose their bodily functions when I tried helping them get up from where they passed out during intercourse. Then there were the sailors who roughly handled me when they mistook me for a lady of the evening, but I never felt the sense of foreboding permeating a space as I did in that house of horrors at the far end of Goodman's Fields. I know that feeling from all the places where the Ripper strangled and carved up women.

I tell the driver our address, and Henry jumps up next to me. "Utterson is now well acquainted with his client Edward Blackwell and his wife, Caroline. They, along with Clarence Collier, attend Trinity Paddington. Utterson no longer sits on vestry there. Utterson will make inquiries about Burrough and her house of infants in the courts and government. He is doing his due diligence on behalf of a client."

"I wouldn't put it past Mrs. Burrough to check on us."

"Tonight, please be sure to tell Collier he is a vestryman who attends the early services after his shift is over," Henry says.

The ride is short. "Let's check on Lucy," I say. My thoughts are on babies, missing babies, dead babies, unwanted babies, and the babies I may not conceive.

"I gave Utterson instructions to contact my father's long-time shipping agent to make the inquiries about Lucy's mother at the ports. The agent is to handle this matter directly and immediately on behalf of Utterson's unnamed and well-paying client. "

Poole greets us at the door. "A Mr. Paddy McCreary is waiting for you in the kitchen. He would have missed his dinner, but the ladies fed him some of the wonderful cakes and shortbreads."

"Have you sampled any?" Henry asks.

Poole blushes, "Maybe one, sir."

I brush the crumbs from his vest.

We make our way to the kitchen. We both stop at the wash-basin to wash our hands and wipe our brows. The ladies are still up to their elbows in flour, busily checking on pies, cakes, and cookies in the oven. A large pot of lamb stew is on the top burner. Next to it on a cutting board is a fresh loaf of bread. I greet them, and they take turns telling us about today's progress. Paddy stands to greet us.

Louise pulls me aside first. "It's Alice."

"What's wrong?" I say, sending the second word into a higher octave.

"Nothing, the opposite and that concerns me."

We both stare at Alice pressing a cookie cutter into dough. She is totally absorbed in the process. Sally is next to her, rocking Lucy. I want to reach for the baby. It is the first time since the alley I wanted to hold her. Really hold her.

"How many days does it usually take for our women to stop craving alcohol?" Louise asks.

We have witnessed dozens try and fail. This dozen has made it through each day: shakes, horrible dreams, no appetite, mood swings, thoughts of death by suicide and searing headaches. With Henry's remedies, the withdrawal symptoms have not been as severe. "Has she partaken of the remedy?" I ask.

"Not a drop. She is showing none of the usual signs. She falls asleep quickly and is up before all of us to check on the baby," Louise says. We both watched Alice become a slave to the devil's drink, staggering about, sleeping rough, soiling herself and debasing herself with the men taking her up on her lewd offerings.

Henry is conferring with Paddy, both of them sampling a shortbread.

"Can her purpose since the morning she saved the baby be so powerful and all-consuming that it is burning the gin out of her being?" I ask.

"Seen nothing like this," Louise says.

"She is focused on the tasks on hand from waking until she closes her eyes. We must be careful when this becomes routine for her. Is she acting possessive of the baby?" I ask without tipping my hand.

"No more than the other ladies, me included." Louise smiles. Louise is the first woman I successfully rescued from the streets. Both of us are acutely aware of withdrawal symptoms.

I move over to the other side of Sally. "May I hold the baby?" Sally hands her over to me. I clutch her to my bosom. The sensation is like no other. The activity in the room, the chatter, the smells all give way to the sensation of this waking infant reaching her mouth to my nipple.

"The milk is cool enough now." Sally hands me the bottle, and I brush the opening to the baby's lips with my finger, and she follows it to the bottle. I paid close attention when the others did that. It is the first time in my entire life I have fed a baby. I was the youngest in my parent's house. I was never asked to care for neighbor's infants. Mary McCreary's youngest were running and jumping around before she pulled me from the third ring of Dante's Inferno.

If God created a better feeling, God kept in heaven. The feeling of Lucy nestling against my breast while I feed her. She takes the bottle hungrily. But then fiery feelings, like lava from the center of the earth, buried in my womb, burst forth and crash into my voice box. So strong is the rush, I can only stifle it with all my inner-strength and I thrust baby and bottle to Louise before rushing off to the coolness of the basement. I land on both knees and cover my mouth with hands and muffle the screams of loss for my baby boy and my marriage. My buried past exploding like the top off a dormant volcano.

LUCKY LEADS me to the basement. The ladies told me to give Francine some time. They understand better what was the matter than this old bachelor, who spent decades focused on dealing with the libertine and vulgar Mr. Hyde. Do I have what is needed to console Francine? Do I have the stamina to keep up with a young wife and baby? I carry three bowls of the stew, as many hunks of warm bread, two cups of water and Lucky's water bowl. With each unsteady step, more water sloshes onto the tray, soaking the bread. With a better appreciation for servants who carry more up and down flights of steps without spilling a drop, I reach the bottom step and see her huddled on the floor. As my eyes adjust to the darkness, I see she is sleeping fitfully. "Francine," I whisper. Nothing.

Our pooch wastes no time licking her salty cheeks and nudges her chin with his. She wakes slowly and pets his head and sits up against the unused coal furnace in this section of the house. I sit cross-legged across from her and set out our bowls. Lucky waits until Francine says, "Eat, Lucky," and he flies to his bowl. She breaks up pieces of his hunk of bread and dips them into her stew before placing them on the sterling silver serving tray. She watches him finish his meal. He cuddles next to her thigh.

"My baby boy would have been walking now. Who knows what would have become of my marriage if I hadn't miscarried and drowned my sorrows in a stolen bottle of Irish whiskey." Her voice is hoarse from crying, and I point to her cup.

"Only the best water for you, Francine."

She drinks "How is Lucy?"

"Asleep."

"The ladies must have thought I lost my mind."

"They knew from the minute you brought her home; it was stirring up feelings you had buried. Your mission has been helping them and women like them. They said you avoided holding her because it would bring up those feelings."

"Their words?" She savors the first bite of stew.

"Their words and more," I say. "You know better than I, Francine, the insights and clarity a woman who frees herself from alcohol can have. Suddenly, fuzzy concepts, like objects on a foggy London morn, become crystal clear in the light of sobriety."

Her appetite returns. Lucky repositions himself against her for a chance to nap with his mistress. We eat in silence. Until she is almost finished and looks at up at me and asks suddenly. "Paddy?"

I finished swallowing and answered. "Not much from Mary McCreary. Her store and that horrid house are as far apart as you can get in Whitechapel. Burrough is British and doesn't hire Irish. Nobody wants to talk to Mary about unwed mothers having babies; the shame is too great. Mary isn't giving up, but she will need to loosen up some tongues."

"What did you tell him?" she asks me.

"We both had a bad feeling about the house, our impression of Mrs. Burrough, her daughter and what the setup was like."

"The wet nurses?"

"I didn't ask," I am sorry. I should have thought about them. "They come and go. We should try to find them?"

"The empty crib?"

"Yes. I did tell him we thought that was Rosie's baby's crib. He said he would tell his mother all this."

She nodded absentmindedly. Did she want an excuse to see her husband and show Rosie she had done what was asked of her? "Is there still some chocolate cake left?"

"In the kitchen," I said.

She woke Lucky from his snuggle and stood on shaky legs. "I need to change and will meet you there in a few minutes. I want to check on the women and our baby."

———

I GO to wash my face again and change my clothes. The house of horrors needs to be removed from my physical being. I quickly pry up the floorboard in my bedroom, where I keep my keepsake box. I pad downstairs in my nightgown and stockings. The ladies have retired for the evening. Louise hugs me good night before turning down her reading lamp. She stayed awake for my sake. Lucy is sleeping in her crib. What was in the past cannot be changed. I can only change the future. I stare at a cherub from heaven. My God-sent cherub. From my pocket, I withdraw a pair of knitted baby socks and slip them on. They were to be my son's. I will tell the women in the morning, so they know the socks are special. I greet Henry in the kitchen with a hug, smile, and an appetite for cake. Maybe someday the appetite will be for him.

13

Agatha and Jane approach me after breakfast.

"Francine, we would like a moment."

They have been with me the longest after Louise. Neither show any interest in accompanying me on my nightly forays into Whitechapel. Something to do with the call of the Sirens. I fully understand. Henry's garden is a perfect place for a stand-up meeting. I am struck by the cold, damp air pressing down on us. I regret leaving the warmth and smells of the kitchen without our hats and coats. Lucky scurries about the enclosed area, making sure no rats or cats have intruded on his master's property overnight. I am sure they want to comfort me. They last saw me running from them in tears.

"We've an idea and want your approval."

A joyful surprise. I encourage them to continue with a tilt of my head. Both are young, healthy now, and a sparkle has returned to their eyes — the devil has released the death grip on their minds and throats. They help the newer arrivals and burn off their growing energy in the kitchen.

"We'd like to sell Sally's baked goods in the market to help pay for our keep and to use the profits for New Hope." They wait for my response with bated breath.

"Tell me more," I say. The idea has merit for both reasons, and I think they are ready.

"We would start with a cart and then wait for a stall to become free."

"Go on."

"The delivery people and workers who come to the house have sampled the goods and tell us they would pay good money." Both women know only too keenly what men will pay good money for.

"I see."

"The cakes and pies alone would fly off the shelves immediately."

"Especially when you give them some cookies for the children for free," I say. I learned that from Mary McCreary.

"Free samples too." Jane says. Their smiles are as wide as London Bridge, both acutely aware of what a free taste can do to whet the appetite.

"Do you think we can send some cookies and scones down to Mary McCreary's store?" I ask.

"What should we charge her?" Jane asks.

"Nothing," Agatha replies. "You know what Mrs. McCreary has done for Francine."

"Of course," Jane says. "My mistake."

I have told my story to each woman countless times. 'As Mary McCreary told me' starts many of my conversations. You would think I am quoting from a saint in the Bible. "As long as she sells them in a bag with New Hope Bakery stamped on them," I say.

"Word of mouth selling," Jane says.

"More like taste in mouth selling." Agatha giggles. They share a ribald sense of humor from their brief careers on the streets.

"That's a fair trade," Jane says. "And the address of our new location when it's ready."

"Yes, our new address." So much has happened in the past few days. Finding the baby. Meeting Seamus. Actually, talking with Rosie. Henry and I making plans with Utterson. Jousting with Mrs. Burrough. Have I forgotten about the new home for New Hope?

Lucky would stay outside all day if I let him, but it's time for us to return to the warmth. I call him, and he comes. "Let's go inside and tell the ladies," I say.

With these baking skills, I can see many of our ladies offering samples to households where full-time bakers are needed, far away from the gin palaces and saloons of Whitechapel. I waited until it was their idea. Since the day I sampled one of Sally's desserts in my cramped flat, I could see the possibilities. Get the women off the street to a safe place with other sober women, build up their self-esteem, talk about the future, and now teaching them a skill in our ovens they could take anywhere and send them out into the world with a new skill and a new hard-earned identity.

Agatha and Jane are ready. They are so excited to share the news. Both women announce the decision. The others were in on the secret and greet them with whoops and hugs. Henry arrives just in time to see the celebration.

"What's all this?" he says.

"Do you think our holding company can support another venture?" I ask.

He listens to the chatter for a minute or two. "New Hope Bakery." He smiles. "By all means. I will talk to Utterson at the club tonight."

"Dining out?" I ask.

"Yes. A few doctors are members who may shed more light on that shady adoption house. I want to find out who makes regular visits there. With so many infants coming and going, I have to think some would be in need."

"Ask them who visits women in the immediate area having just given birth for a likely list of wet nurses," I say.

"Yes, I keep forgetting about the nurses," he says.

An idea foments in my mind the minute I utter those words to him. "I need to run an errand in my best clothes," I say.

"Where to, pray tell?" he asks.

"Scotland Yard."

He stands back with a wary look on his face.

"No, not that vulgar Newcomen. I will impose on the Inspector handling the Ripper investigation for a favor."

My response does little to undo Doctor Jekyll's worried brow.

"INSPECTOR ABBERLINE, thank you for seeing me without an appointment," I say.

"Mrs. Murphy, I can always spare a few minutes for you." He is tall with thick curly black hair and an equally thick moustache flowing into mutton chop sideburns. His suit is a sharp brown tweed and appears freshly pressed.

I am puzzled by his greeting.

"I am grateful for your advice. We are slowly putting together a sketch of Jack from the cabbies and ladies of the night frequenting the quadrangle of blocks where he committed four of the five atrocities."

Blushing, I reply. "Your instruction to the constables is apparent to me nightly. I go about my rounds, talking with the women they encounter, and I have not heard of a single complaint."

"Yes, I have since learned of your mission. You are to be

commended for your selfless service to the most disadvantaged members of the community."

Not to be outdone offering genuine praise. "The streets are safer thanks to your efforts." I know the true reason the Ripper has not struck again, but the streets are safer with the extra patrols.

"You are too kind," he says. It is his turn to blush. "How can I help you?"

"My estranged husband's sister left her infant in the care of Mrs. Burrough, who lives at the desolate end of Goodman's Fields. Rosie returned the following day to make the last payment before setting sail to America and found the baby was missing. She told me she had notified the police."

"How does a baby go missing?"

"Someone must have taken the baby, or Mrs. Burrough adopted the infant boy out or..."

Abberline finishes my sentence. "The baby is dead and was disposed of."

I don't want to admit that possibility. "Having met Mrs. Burrough, I cannot discount it. I went there with an older gentleman posing as an interested couple who cannot conceive."

He smiled. "An interesting ruse, I must admit. I will find the report and speak with the constable."

"Would it be worthwhile to ask former employees of Mrs. Burrough and the wet nurses who came to the house about the goings on there?" I earned his respect from the advice I gave him following the last inquest into the Ripper's handiwork. "At best, the baby was prematurely adopted out with the house matron, thinking its mother would not be returning to settle her debt. At worst, the child was kidnapped or killed."

"I will interview the constable who took the report and give him your advice verbatim," he says.

"Thank you, Inspector Abberline."

"You are most welcome, Mrs. Murphy."

As I take my leave from his office, I place my hand on the doorknob, turn and say. "Constable Clarence Collier is doing a fine job on his rounds. Tell him I appreciate his efforts. A young woman died giving birth in an alley and she possessed no identification save a piece of paper with an address on it. On his own time, he visited that address. We were about to go in when he came out."

"The same address?"

I nod, and his eyes widen.

"Shall I ask him to see you in the morning, sir?"

"By all means, Mrs. Murphy and the baby?"

"We are taking care of it in the West End. A healthy girl."

"Of course. I will talk to him about both matters."

"Thank you, Inspector." I leave him to work on the crime of the century and place two more items on his plate. How is the house connected to both Rosie and the unidentified woman? Were they both going there to leave their babies? What is the common thread in their misfortune?

I choose to walk the distance from The Yard to Cavendish Square. Answers come to me when I walk. The air is heavy and not fresh. London has used the Thames as its toilet for centuries, and the wind carries the stench along my route. Houses are shuttered, and front gardens show no signs of happiness. The gaiety of the Christmas season is not upon us yet. The thick grey clouds should just rain and send the accumulation of horse droppings and urine on the cobblestones into the sewers. I have no reason to be distracted, no smiling faces, no vendors hawking fruit from southern climes. I try to add pieces to the puzzle I just laid out for Abberline whilst I stuff my feelings for Seamus and about Rosie back where they belong.

14

Henry, Louise, and I meet her in the garden. The stench from the river, along with soot from the factories, leaves a sour taste in my mouth. She shows remarkable calm and displays a resolute manner. Louise and I exchange glances. None of the women have given up her reason for wanting to meet us this morning. She is taller than the others and stronger too. They ask her to reach for things in the top cupboards and to help carry laundry from the basement. Her black hair still shows signs of drink ravaging her body, but she has washed it and done her best to make it presentable. She could find clothes that fit her. Her outfit was a West End church lady's clothes before they were sold in an estate auction. I barely had time to advise Henry about my conversation with Inspector Abberline when Alice Hardy came to Louise with a request.

"Is this about the baby?" I ask. I dread the thought of her wanting to raise Lucy as her own. I can understand her attachment after she saved the baby's life in that squalid alley.

"Both babies, actually. Why are they connected to the house at the ass end of Goodman's Fields? Pardon my French," she says. She knows the basics, but we have not shared all the details with anyone else except Louise.

"We are still trying to puzzle it out," Henry says. "Francine's former husband's sister left her baby boy there and returned a day later to find him missing."

I give the man credit for providing the information. Becoming my former husband was a choice Seamus made. Mary McCreary helped me look forward and not back. After almost three years, Mr. Murphy seeks me out for help? What if I were to find Rosie's baby, would he want me back? Does that make me good enough for him? With Rosie in New York or Boston, our marriage would not be under daily assault from her sharp tongue and disdainful stares. Could we start over again? Could we try to start a family? Is Henry trying to make it sound like Seamus is out of the picture by calling him my former husband? Wealthy Londoners can get divorces. Poor Irish Catholics commit a sin if they divorce. My energies are channeled into helping Whitechapel's unfortunates regain their sanity and start a new life. Have I started a new life where I don't need to meet the approval of Mr. Murphy?

I say, "The police found a slip of paper in the dead woman's coat pocket with the same address on it. They think she was robbed of her purse and got lost trying to find the location. She may be from Holland from the type of shoes she was wearing."

"Has anybody filed a missing person's report?" Alice asks.

"No, but I am trying to get Scotland Yard involved, and maybe the constable Sally dragged to the alley. He has done some follow-up on his own time. We saw him come out of the house," I say.

"He didn't know about your sister-in-law's missing child?" Alice asks.

I shake my head and say, "But he knows now, and I will ask him tonight to visit the Inspector I spoke with to see if he is interested in looking into both matters. The police have their hands full looking for Jack."

"Did you go into the house?" she asks.

"A young woman married to an aging playboy toured the set-up. They were looking to adopt a boy," Henry answered.

"And?" she asked.

I tell her what we saw. She asks a few questions to clarify what I remember. Henry answers with his opinions too.

"Why are you interested, Alice?" Louise asks.

"I have some skills with babies from my previous life. I lived in a small village up north, and the doctor was not always able to help the women. Then..."

"What?" Louise asks.

"The army called him to India, and he never returned—an Afghan bullet to the head."

"Your husband?" Henry asks. He breaks a rule about not asking about the past. We focus on the future, but I am realizing from my experience that stuffing those unresolved feelings deep into my heart is not a permanent solution. They can come out without warning. I thought I was doing fine until Seamus found me in front of Ten Bells Pub the other morning.

She nods. That far-off stare Louise and I have seen many times with the women who return to the streets. Are we going to lose Alice? She shakes off the memories like they were the rain on her head and shoulders from a cloudburst that evening before we heard the screams. "I came to London to work for a wealthy family when the nanny quit abruptly. I needed a fresh start. Three babies in three years and the young wife was incapable of managing the household. I took on more responsibilities except servicing the man of the house."

Louise said, "What happened in that house sent you to us, but not right away. We understand."

Tears formed in Alice's eyes. "When we saved that baby's life,

I knew then and there it was the right time to say yes to Francine. I want to help you now, and I think I know how."

We listen as she proffers an idea. Louise asks her directly if the plan fails, will she go back to the street. "I know where to go if the sirens call me. I can steer away from the rocks and find safe harbor here."

"What do you need?" Henry asks.

"Rooms nearby, a trunk of clothes, and a fresh reference."

We work out more details.

"How will I get messages to you?" Alice asks.

"You know how to find Mary McCreary's store?" I ask.

She nods.

"Ask Paddy to deliver your messages," I say.

Louise says, "A message every day, Alice. If you miss one day. Every woman in this building will be scouring Whitechapel for you. We don't want to lose you to the streets. The New Hope Mission is to restore women to sanity and to give them a future. I don't want us," looking directly at Henry and I, "to lose sight of that. We can't help that poor girl who died while giving birth. We are taking care of her baby for now. It is fine we help Rosie O'Sullivan's baby, but remember two things about the Murphys. We don't owe them a damn thing."

"And the second?" I ask.

"They are the reason New Hope was formed in the first place and why we are taking a chance with losing another woman to the streets. Because suddenly Francine, who they discarded like yesterday's garbage, can now help them."

"Tell us how you really feel, Louise?" I ask, trying to take control of the meeting. I feel gut punched, not from a sense Louise is being disloyal, but from the truth. Louise has proved her loyalty to me, but always when it came to saving the mission. She is pointing out that I have veered from the mission to find out how the foundling house is connected to Lucy and Baby James.

"I owe you my life, Francine, but these babies are taking you away from your mission. Tell me to stuff it and I won't utter another word."

"You are probably right," I say. "Can you help Henry and I with all the details of making New Hope a reality? I can't turn my back on a promise I made to both of them."

"Both of whom?" she asks.

"The baby Alice saved, and the baby Rosie gave away."

"Not the Murphys." It is more of a demand than a question.

I avoid the question and ask her again, "Will you help us with the details?"

Louise replies, "I am sorry we had this conversation in front of Alice and Dr. Jekyll, but I don't want to lose this woman to the hell we all know too well."

I look at Henry. He has been through hell too. It's not too late to tell Alice I made a hasty decision. Louise knows we are stretched with the babies and the baking. "I am not the reason New Hope is within our grasp. You are the reason, Louise Anderson. You have been there on the mission every step of the way. When I stumbled, you were there to pick me up. When it was darkest, you asked for Dr. Jekyll's help when I was too stubborn. Can I rely on you until I can devote my full attention to our mission?" Admitting to others how much I rely on Louise is the first time I've said it out loud to her. She deserves better from me.

Lucky barks from the doorway. I look over Louise's shoulder and wave to him. I am sure he sees two women embracing and a man and woman standing nearby, reaching for handkerchiefs.

15

The Gladstone Club on Pall Mall is one of the newer gentlemen's clubs. Its members boast men from all over the British Empire. Old money, new money, retired military, professionals and businessmen who started with nothing more than an idea and the audacity to pursue it. The ivory colored plaster and light blue drapery provides the dining area with the cheery promise of better days ahead. Gold-plated sconces provide gas lighting. No candlesticks to be seen.

Other clubs, with their dark paneling and tobacco-infused leather upholstery, scream of the good old times, which were not so. Gladstone's chef brings together recipes from all over the empire. I am looking forward to my fish and fruit plate recipe from the West Indies, where I recently spent much time unsuccessfully banishing Hyde to the ether. The Jekyll table is endowed by my late father. My guests and I dine without a care in the world about the tab. He made sure it included a fine gratuity for our servers, who trip over themselves to make sure our slightest needs are met.

Samuel Sutton sits to my left and enjoys the olives from his third martini. Albert Blackstone, to my right, busies himself with the last of his salad. The family of the former is old money passed down through several generations; the family of the latter are making a fortune in Canadian lumber. My income is generated by a trust created before my father died two decades ago. The family business is run by a board of directors. The empty chair across from me is where the younger Jekyll brother, George, sat. I tell my tablemates it is unlike George not to have sent a message from his hasty trip to Turkey. He checks on the various holdings of Jekyll Importers. Soon Utterson will receive a telegram from Samsun, Turkey.

I failed him when he was a child. I failed to pay heed to his cries for help during my infrequent visits home from boarding school. I didn't understand his anger towards me until less than a month ago, when I learned he was also abused by my insane mother and her sick, demented lovers; Sir Danvers Carew being one of them.

Newcomen knows why Hyde beat and stomped Carew to death, but not that my brother was also a victim of Carew as well. George's recent hasty trip was easily explained. I've had to view all his bitterness towards me through the lens of this newfound information. I can certainly find it in my heart to forgive him for all misdoings directed at me, save one. Only God can forgive him for the way he dealt with years of sexual, physical and mental abuse.

By New Year's, Sutton and Blackstone will suggest a fourth member for our table—probably an excellent card player with a gift of gab. For now, I must carefully pick the bones from my fish and stare at the empty chair and imagine George, always dapper, prim, and proper, pontificating on the deterioration of moral values in the world's largest city.

My conversation with my associates is rote. I nod and offer asides when needed, but my thoughts drift back to the chaos of the Jekyll household. Nine women, a baby, and a dog are new additions since my return from the islands. Delicious baked treats assault my nostrils morning, noon and night.

Mostly, my thoughts are consumed by Francine Murphy. The talk of babies and her former husband have shown cracks in her steely determination. I find her more attractive than when we first met. Her softer side is endearing. Sometimes, I want to hold her in my arms, the way she held me on the docks that morning. Often before daylight, when I know she is but a door knock away, and the others would never know how we might express our intimate yearnings, I listen quietly until she awakens. It is not for me to knock on her door. All trust would fly out the window as fast as the contents of a Whitechapel chamber pot. Not only has Hyde flooded me with memories, from the time I was five years old, but also his randy explorations of London where respectable West End gentlemen's boots dare not tread. My libido is in full gallop when I smell her hair or when we pet Lucky and our hands touch. These feeling are unlike anything I have ever experienced before in my five decades on this earth. Dare I speak to her about this surge of emotions? I tell her about memories Hyde stored when he protected me from all the horrors of my upbringing. Do I explain in the sonorous tones of a doctor making a diagnosis of the lust Hyde hid from me all those years? Just as she is ill-prepared to deal with her past when her former husband finds her, I am trying to maintain the appearance of respected physician while Hyde's libertine nature inhabits my heart's desires like a bagful of cats.

———

BRANDY AND CIGARS are next in the smoking lounge. Sutton is soused. Blackstone, not so much. I scan the room and settle on a table where two of London's best surgeons are in heated debate.

"...the Frenchman doesn't have the faintest clue what he is talking about," Dr. Maxwell Smith says.

"But the facts speak for themselves. His paper passes rigorous inspection," Dr. Samuel Cleworth replies.

Dr. Smith volleys back. "Neither of us have seen him in the operating theater. I will withhold judgment until I see it with my own two eyes."

"You are the churchgoer Smith. What does the gospel say of the apostle Thomas with his doubts?"

I interrupt their debate at that junction of God and medicine. "A moment of your time, if I may, for a quick question."

"Yes, Jekyll, by all means, Cleworth is as quick with his wits as he is with his scalpel, and I am afraid his passion for this subject will cut me to the bone," Dr. Smith says.

"Both of you, are held in high regard in all of London. Might you know the names of doctors caring for children and infants in Whitechapel?"

"None who will admit to it, I am afraid," Dr. Cleworth responds. Both doctors chuckle.

"Why is that?" I ask.

"You are known as a respected chemist with a practice in the West End. How much would you expect to be paid in Whitechapel? We think your expenses would exceed your income quickly."

"Charity wards?" I prod.

"Attached to the hospitals nearby. No doctor that I know makes house visits," Dr. Smith smugly folds his arms.

"Midwives and nurses mostly make house calls there. They buy their supplies here and mark them up," Dr Cleworth adds.

"When a man gets injured?"

"That's different. Employers have doctors on call if the man is worth it."

"So, I might check with businesses and factories to learn who their on-call physicians are?

They nod. "You can ask the midwives too if they know of any doctors making the rounds of Whitechapel. Good luck, Jekyll." Cleworth smiles smugly and returns to face Smith. Our conversation is over.

Strangely, they didn't seem in the least bit interested in why I wanted this information. Was it because I was asking about the poorest, crime-ridden, rat-infested section of London? I think it is because no respectable doctor would traipse there to treat a patient with little or no means to pay them for their services. Somehow, treating the denizens of Whitechapel would reflect on their worth. They would be seen as second-rate doctors. Smith and Cleworth would have to fight for their exorbitant fees with the well-heeled families in the tonier section of town if word got out they were slumming it.

I return to my table where Sutton is snoozing, and Blackwell is trying unsuccessfully to relight his cigar. The surgeons are back in their debate with fervor. They didn't seem to want to engage me in conversation, and I wasn't the least bit interested in who the Frenchman was or what they found so important. I never had to worry about where my money came from. My father provided me with West End wealth. It was only my attraction to Francine Murphy that brought me to Whitechapel. What if I had to work to put food on the table and a roof over my head?

About the doctors working in Whitechapel to make ends meet, borrowing from the Gospel again, who was I to cast the first stone?

16

"We should find Constable Collier first," I tell Sally. "We've received no word from the shipping agent yet."

"He promised he would provide you with a sketch of the poor girl. That should help," Sally replied.

I am excited to tell him about my conversation with Inspector Abberline. Excited for Collier that he can do some actual detective work, and excited for us that the police are involved in both matters at the Burroughs house.

Louise was right to dress me down about my preoccupation with babies. Although in my defense, we rescued an infant from certain death, and I was asked by my husband, whom I had not spoken with for nearly three years, to intercede on his sister's behalf.

Collier spots us as he turns the corner by the Ten Bells Pub. The night is clear, but cold. North winds warn us of an icy winter coming. The half-moon is playing hide and seek with grey silver-lined clouds.

"Mrs. Murphy," he says. He tips his cap to Sally. "Ma'am."

"We've got a dozen blueberry muffins, and I'm sure one has

your name on it," I say. The aroma from the open basket is arresting. The large man moves towards it like a bloodhound. "Pick one."

"You are very gracious, ladies. I ate an early supper with the missus. She had to visit a sick sister. He selects one and half of it disappears in his cavernous maw.

While he chews with a blissful look on his face, I ask, "Any luck with the sketch?"

He swallows. "Should be done tomorrow." The remaining half disappears as quickly as the first.

"We've received no word from our source on the docks about the poor girl yet."

"I will be the first you tell if you do," he says.

"That is our agreement," I say.

"We are bad for business," Sally says. "The men see you and want to disappear."

"And that's a bad thing?" Collier asks. "I wish we could put a man in front of every gin palace and pub in Whitechapel. It would cut down on the obvious, but also the robberies and drunken brawls."

In my time helping the unfortunate women of the street, I've seen plenty of both instances.

"As my mammie would say, 'nothing good happens after midnight.'" Collier says.

I say, "That reminds me, Constable Clarence Collier, the older gentleman and young woman you met in front of the horrible house in Goodman's Field are Edward and Caroline Blackwell. We three attend the early service at Trinity Paddington if Mrs. Burrough should ask. You sit on the Vestry there."

"Tell me more," he says.

"We pretended to be a barren couple looking to adopt a boy to keep the Blackwell lineage intact. The second floor held cribs for the boys. Each crib had a future date written on a card, and there was a star next to each one."

"What did you make of that?" he asks.

"The date is when the boy will be available for adoption, and the star signified the baby was already claimed for adoption. The last crib by the backstairs was empty. The date scheduled was a year from the day Rosie left Baby James there. We think that was his crib."

"Good detective work, Mrs. Murphy."

"The boys look well cared for by at least one cheerful nurse." I close my eyes and take a deep breath. I can tell Collier senses my apprehension.

"But?"

"On the third floor, the girls are kept. All were asleep, and the nurse told us she keeps them 'comfortable'. All had dates, but only a few had stars. It made me realize that if the unidentified dead woman found the Burrough house, Lu—the baby girl we found might have been in one of those cribs. It was very disturbing."

"And the half-wit?"

"Felicity is her name. She runs errands for the nurses. She is in her own world. She was reciting a nursery rhyme while we inspected the premises."

"What do you think happens to the girls when the time on their card arrives?" he asks.

I look from his face up into the sky. The moon ducks behind a thicker cloud, and we are cast in a dark pall. I shudder and pull my coat tighter to my throat and chest.

"I spoke to Inspector Abberline this morning about the goings on there."

Collier steps back and says, "Abberline is in charge of the Ripper investigation; he has no time for this missing dead girl and missing baby."

"He told me as much, and that is when I suggested you."

"You what?" Collier appears startled and leans on his back foot.

"I told him you followed up at the Burrough house on your own time about the scrap of paper in the dead woman's possession."

"Ah Jaysus, Mrs. Murphy, I wish you hadn't done that. I went off my beat to do that. I could be in trouble. I should have passed the note on to a day man for follow-up."

Sally looks at her shoes first and then slowly moves away to give us more privacy.

"Abberline didn't see it that way at all. He suggested you meet with him in the morning. He could arrange for you to take over both investigations. You would like that, wouldn't you?"

"Mrs. Murphy, it is not for you to say what I would like. I work for the Metropolitan Police. My commander may not see things the same way you and I do. I did that on the sly. I may get into trouble."

I move in closer, and he doesn't retreat. I look straight into his chest. "Clarence, you are a good man. You treat people with respect, even when they may be at their worst. You are smart, and you care. I would not have taken Abberline into my confidence if I thought it would cause you any harm." I look into his eyes. "Meet Abberline in the morning and maybe tomorrow night you will be home in a nice warm bed." The moon breaks out of the clouds and shines on our faces. I can tell he is indecisive. "You've been invited to Scotland Yard, Constable Collier." I turn to Sally and reach into the basket for two more muffins. "Bring Frederick my gift and my salutations."

———

I NEED the cold air to clear my senses. Brandy and cigars fogged my brain. Blackwell hails a cab for us, but I demur, choosing instead to walk. Sutton revived as he often does and joined a few of the other members around the piano for songs and gaiety. Much money and no purpose can do that to a man.

It was not a surprise to learn that the residents of Whitechapel did not have enough doctors to go around. Most of their care took place at the hospitals when their conditions worsened. It is as if nothing has changed since we walked out of caves. It is up to the women to take care of the women and children. Forget churches or government. It depends on women helping women, whether it is what Francine is doing at night or Burrough is doing, although her motives are unclear. It is what I learned after I spoke with surgeons that surprised me.

Surprisingly, it was the fellow with sanitation planning who filled me in. Fetuses and babies found in the sewer lines throughout London expose the desperation of having another mouth to feed. A woman without the means to pay for a proper burial of a stillborn or premature birth that doesn't make it discards their child into the sewers for the flow to take them to the Thames and then to the sea. A modern city, yet a solution not much different from when we were roving tribes. But it was this city bureaucrat who provided me with information Utterson might be able to use and what I won't share with Francine until I know if my hunch is correct.

I have walked this path from Gladstone to my home so many times that I lost count. Carriages and hansoms ply their trade as concerts and plays are now letting out. Laughter and excited chatter of the leisure class surround me as I turn to the corner to Cavendish Square. I spot a cab in front of my abode. Is it Francine? Is she bringing home another unfortunate? Might she and I share a treat with our dog in the privacy of my bedchamber? My excitement increases with my pace as I approach the cab. Why is she not alighting?

Suddenly, a familiar figure alights from the interior. I hear Lucky barking from inside my residence. He is warning me.

"Dr. Jekyll," he says. A burly constable ambles behind him.

"Inspector Newcomen, to what do I owe the pleasure?"

17

Paddy's note says Dorothy Jones lives on the third floor on the right in the rear. He arrives just in time to sit with a half dozen fawning women for breakfast. Henry, Louise and I discuss the contents. We hatch a plan. He and Louise will go to the New Hope future site to meet an architect for the interior build-out. Henry reminds me that once the title changes hands, demolition and reconfiguring can start, but accurate measurements are needed first. The agent for the owner was happy to provide us with a key, a juicy sales commission in the offing.

Our cab drops me first on Brick Street. The cabbie and his horse both snort in disapproval at the decrepit building. This tenement on Brick Street is indistinguishable from the others on that side of the road. It sits ugly and backlit in the pale December morning sun. Three stories of faded brown with peeling white trim wood frame. There are four flats on each floor. The front steps and interior stairwell are not to tread quickly in either direction. Smells of greasy cooking, body odor, and mold assault my nostrils.

3R is smudged on the doorframe with a charcoal stick. I

knock and hear a wary, "Whoseit?" emanates from deep behind the cheap wooden door with three sturdy locks.

"Caroline Blackwell," I reply. Henry and I agree the ruse still has its advantages.

"Whadyawant?"

"To settle an account in your favor," I answer.

The door flies open immediately. She is younger than I imagined. Reddened hands, nails bitten to the quick. The color of her skin bleached out up to her elbows. The housedress is tired but clean. Strawberry blond hair listlessly frames a thin face, pale lips and coal-black eyes squinting hard into the poorly sunlit hallway. The hallway windows this high up haven't seen a ladder and sponge in some time. Years of coal dust and smoke from nearby factories smudge the glass, giving the hallway a dusty haze.

"My name is Caroline Blackwell. My husband and I have been to the foundling house. We wish to adopt a boy. I am not impressed with Mrs. Burrough, but she has plenty of boys to choose from."

"What's that have to do with me?"

"You were the laundress, and I understand you weren't treated well. Your last payment was short. I am prepared to make up the difference, but I need to know what goes on there."

"Why not ask her for references?" she asks.

"If we received a boy from her, we wouldn't want someone asking us about our dealings there. Here's why. My husband and I plan to go abroad, possibly to France or the Spanish coast, and return with our child. No one would be the wiser we adopted a boy. She owes you how much?"

"I don't know if I like this very much."

"My husband can put in a good word for you in the West End. A good laundress is scarce."

"How would that work?"

"A letter of reference for Dorothy Jones with the names of

several families who might be interested. I hope that is suffi-cient, Dorothy."

She smiles. "Call me Dottie."

I smile back. "What can you tell me, Dottie?"

"She owed me almost two quid." To make it obvious, one hand holds the door while the other reaches out, palm up.

I turn aside and unclasp my purse. She needs not see the contents or be able to snatch it from my hand. I withdraw the money and hand it to her. "No need to give me back the differ-ence." I smile.

She pockets the coins in a flash.

I cock my head and arch my eyes with a puzzled look.

Dottie says, "Mrs. Burrough is a hard woman. She will tell you she was widowed, but her husband left her after their daughter was found to be…"

"Felicity," I interrupt.

She nods as I just filled in the awkward silence.

"Please continue."

"She puts advertisements in the papers to board babies for up to a year. She takes boys in for adoption with a list of prospective families wanting to adopt. It works well when there are more couples than children, but that hasn't been the case in recent years."

"How so?"

"There are more houses like hers offering to place babies for lower prices. Her house needs more repairs, and she must pay her hired help. And…"

"There are more babies than families who want to adopt," I finish her sentence. The economics of buying and selling chil-dren. A war was fought in America to abolish the selling of slaves, but here, she can publicize the buying and selling of babies. All perfectly legal, all perfectly accepted. Of course, like the slaves, babies have no say in the bartering. In desperate times, what can the mothers say when they are with no means?

She nods again.

"Every morning I would arrive in the laundry with dozens of soiled nappies and bedclothes to wash. During the day, her daughter would fly down the stairs repeating those silly rhymes and hand me a full basket. This was my work six days a week. Before I quit, Mrs. Burrough was not replacing the nappies with newer ones. Money was tight. She stretched out my payments to the breaking point. When she did buy new nappies, a new one was put on a boy while the adoptive parents waited in the parlor, fresh swaddling clothes too. It was like she was giving them a present."

"Any girls?" I had to ask.

"Only when Burrough could convince the couple the boy and girl were brother and sister."

"Was that true?"

Dottie shrugged. "More money for Burrough made everyone in the house happier."

"Did you get to know any of the nurses who don't work there anymore?"

"I might have." Dottie looked at my purse.

"Any of the wet-nurses?"

"Refresh my memory." She licked her bottom lip and bit it.

"Any reason my husband and I should not adopt a boy from her?"

She answered immediately. "None, the boys were well cared for."

"What about the need for doctors when the boys got sick?"

"There was one. I didn't know his name. Older man from India. Limped. I think he had a wooden leg and—" She looked away.

"What, Dottie?" I asked.

"He would pronounce the girls dead when one of them didn't wake up."

"Did that happen often?" I asked softly.

"Mondays were the hardest." Her eyes welled up. She started to close the door on me.

"I can come back with a letter of reference and a client list. Would you like that?"

She sniffed and barely nodded. "All those girls."

I knew better than to knock on the closed door staring me in the face.

Carefully walking down the dimly lit stairs and out onto the street, I don't need a map to get to the future home of New Hope. My feet know these streets. I watch as children play, running back and forth, laughing and shrieking in whatever games they make up. My focus in this part of town has been on the women who have lost their way. Rarely do I think of the boys and girls who survive and who live in this abject poverty.

My thoughts keep returning to Lucy, who slept in my arms after her feeding this morning. A baby girl. A precious baby girl. Not a commodity to be bought and sold. A baby her mother never held.

An idea forms in my mind. Louise would chide me. Lucky wouldn't mind. Lucy would approve, but what about Henry? Thoughts of Rosie and Seamus fade. I want to find Baby James because, because why? Is it to be in their good graces? No, that isn't quite it. Is it to find myself back in my husband's muscular arms again? I can't deny that feeling, but that isn't quite it either. Do I want to adopt Baby James so Lucy can have a brother? Rosie isn't coming back, I am sure. Seamus will not want me to dump his nephew on his doorstep either. He would have been fine with being called Uncle Seamus if O'Sullivan was still alive, but now? My reasons for finding Baby James don't bubble to the surface of my mind, but there is a burning desire to do so.

I shake myself out of my daydreams to see the architect talking with Louise and Henry on the street. Two cabs pointing in different directions, their horses indifferent to the conversation taking place, their cabbies, don't mind idling their time as a good tip awaits them both.

"Dr. Jekyll," I call out. Always a gentleman, he helped Louise into the carriage first. I skip across the street. Skipping is something I did in County Cork. Skipping is something I can teach Lucy. I pretend to skip one extra step, and I fall into his surprised waiting arms, making him catch me.

I look up into his wide-open eyes and say, "Tell me everything, Henry, and leave nothing out."

18

She asks me to tell her everything, and I am speechless. Is it an accident; Francine falling into my arms? Louise and the driver's backs are turned. Only the horse knows for sure. We quickly disengage, and I help her into the carriage. Is that a saucy shake of the hips or is Hyde making me see things? She sits next to Louise facing me.

"How did your meeting go?" she asks us.

Louise answers first. "The man was thorough. There were some additions and changes to the interior that were not accounted for in the city's plans."

"He made a sketch of the first floor, and we helped hold the measuring strings. Once we have title, we can begin demolition," I say.

"Second floor?"

"It was empty. I paced off space for twenty individual rooms with a common bathroom in the back." Louise is beaming. "We agreed on only twenty," she says, reminding me.

"Third floor. Will it do?" Francine asks.

She nods. This is where Louise will live as the New Hope

house matron. It is plenty spacious enough, with windows on all four sides looking out over rooftops, at church spires and smokestacks. Francine and I first walked these abandoned factory floors before she learned to trust me.

I chuckle at the lie I told her the second time we met. Hyde had placed directions to this very location, a flask of water and a pig's ear next to my doctor's bag. It was his first attempt at communicating with me. I arrived to find a sick and starving dog in the debris of this building's front alcove. As fate or luck would have it, Francine was passing by and saw me ministering to the little canine we later rescued. I told her that a banker from my club said the location was an excellent investment. What an investment it has turned out to be!

"I am happy there is plenty of space for our plans," Francine replies. "More than enough space on the second floor for the ladies, and we can use some of that space for ovens."

"And your morning?" I ask.

"The information Alice passed on to us is accurate. The washwoman didn't get paid her full wages and quit. She told me Mrs. Burrough was having financial difficulties. The woman goes by Dottie. Dottie Jones described the doctor who came to check on the sick babies and the dying ones. She was crying when she recalled all the dead girls and closed the door in my face."

"Did she quit before Rosie's baby went missing?" I ask.

"I don't know. I told her we would provide her with names of housekeepers in the West End in need of a laundress and we would provide her with a letter of reference. I will hold that letter close until she tells me everything she knows."

She looks at me and Louise. "One last thing about the baby Alice saved."

Louise doesn't protest, and neither do I. Satisfied with our silent permissions, she continues. "Sally and I spoke with

Constable Collier last night. At first, he balked at talking with Inspector Abberline this morning, but I am hoping he can see past jurisdictional boundaries and look at this as an opportunity to work on both cases. They are connected to that god-awful house at the end of Goodman's Fields, I know it."

After last night's impromptu visit from a difference inspector, I, for one, would be happier if no police were involved, but that is my problem and one I will not entertain until we are inside our next destination. "We've much to discuss with Utterson," I say and point to his offices.

We are seated immediately in his office by his assistant. Tea is offered and declined. Utterson sweeps in with stacks of papers separated by fingers on both of his hands. He sets them down on his expansive walnut desk in a patchwork manner. Each set of documents cocked at right angles to the one below.

"Allow me to introduce you to Louise Anderson," I say. "It was her brother's desire to have me meet with Mrs. Murphy."

"How do you do, Miss Anderson?" Utterson says.

"Mr. Utterson, the good doctor has said many good things about you," Louise returns the greeting.

I say, "Louise will be working closely with me in the building of the New Hope Mission as Mrs. Murphy has taken on additional responsibilities regarding her former husband's missing nephew."

"Yes, yes, I can understand. On that front, there is much to discuss, but first I have some news from your shipping agent. He has visited a few of the docks and met with the ferry workers as the ships from Rotterdam and Amsterdam were discharging passengers. I am afraid he will need that sketch. Have you spoken with the constable?"

All eyes turn to Francine, who replies, "I should have it tonight, if all goes well."

"Excellent. It will make a difference, I am sure," he says.

"On the sordid matter of warehousing infants, it is as nightmarish as you described, Doctor Jekyll. My sources tell me the house run by Mrs. Burrough is better than most. She has not appeared on the docket since her husband left her, and she sued him to provide care for their daughter. No suits for breach of contract by mothers or by adoptive parents."

Francine spoke up. "I learned today she was not widowed, and that he left her rather than stay in the home with their daughter, Felicity."

"Yes, Felicity is named in the documents." Utterson moves those scant few pages from the top of one pile carefully to the bottom of the other. "I am afraid there is nothing in the courts to give us clues about how the baby disappeared."

"I received a description of a doctor who tends to the children," Francine recites the description given to her by Dottie Jones.

"I will find him and talk to him," I say. "A foreigner with a war wound looking to eke out a practice in London makes sense. The surgeons in my club would avoid Whitechapel like it was plague-infested."

"Much the same for the men in my profession. They meet their Whitechapel clients in court and receive payment before entering their appearance in the docket."

Sitting there with my wealth and West End lawyer reminds me how fortunate I am when he broaches the next subject.

Utterson says, "Newcomen's bluff was exactly that, Henry. No magistrate signed a warrant for Edward Hyde in the murder at Dutfields Yard of Elizabeth Stride."

"What?" both Francine and Louise exclaim simultaneously.

"A man matching Hyde's description was seen running from scene, bleeding profusely from his arm. Newcomen is trying to pin that murder on my former associate," I say, looking straight at Utterson to avoid eye contact with the women. "Newcomen said that because her manner of death differed from the others, the Ripper didn't commit that killing, but the Ripper did kill the woman on Mitre Square along with the three others. Newcomen and the constable, who Edward encountered after midnight, threatened to have me arrested if I didn't produce an address for him. They left Cavendish Square empty-handed when I called their bluff. It was an hour before you and Sally arrived home. I didn't want to concern you. We had more important things to discuss this morning with the note given to Paddy. I sent a messenger to Utterson while you were taking care of the baby."

"Are they saying that Mister Hyde killed 'Long Liz' the same night as the Ripper killed Catherine Eddowes?" Louise asks.

"That was their theory." Luckily I don't have to face Francine as Louise is seated on my other side—next to my tingling arm where the Ripper tried to slash Hyde's throat when Hyde interrupted the Ripper throttling Stride. After that night, I never thought I would see Francine again.

"This is the letter I will send to Newcomen's superiors on your behalf, Henry. I will ask them to suspend him and prevent him from contacting you again. This letter details each time he has harassed you and the time he searched your surgery and found nothing. I just need my assistant to witness your affidavit, and I can send it by a runner immediately."

"We are not notifying the fourth estate about this umbrage," I say.

"No, as you wished. This is only a demand asking for immediate relief." My attorney and closest friend called the assistant in. My signature on the affidavit and two copies were witnessed. Utterson had a busy morning before our arrival. I will talk to Francine privately about Newcomen. He may try to strong arm her if he can't get to me.

"Keep that pen in hand, Doctor Jekyll; you and F. A. Murphy have some additional documents to sign. These are the last steps before we meet with the seller's representatives and the city about finalizing the deal and paying arrearages and fines on the building about to become New Hope Mission".

"Can Louise be a witness on these documents as well?" Francine asks.

"You will need to pass the quill around," Utterson says with a smile.

19

My knock on Dottie Jones's door goes unanswered. Heavy overnight rains postponed my nocturnal travels with Sally in Whitechapel. I slept soundly except for the times I went to peek in on Lucy. The miracle baby took a bottle from me two hours before dawn. I warmed the milk and fed her without dredging up my past and what might have been. Part of me wants Henry to find her family; part of me wants Lucy for us.

I knock again louder, and my exertion is rewarded by the man across the hall opening his door.

"I'm hoping to have a word with Dottie about a few job prospects. D'know where she is off to?"

He sized me up. I smiled.

"Dunno, I thought you were knocking on my door. I work nights as a watchman." He yawned.

I dash off a quick note of the time and place where she can meet me later in the day. I hand him a shilling and the note. "For your troubles. If you could be so kind to give her this, I would be much obliged."

"Yes, mum, I will see to it." My new friend says.

The cobblestones are still slick from the overnight torrential downpour, but the sunshine and clearing breezes from the west give Whitechapel a softer feel. I breathe fresh, clean air deeply with renewed purpose. After signing the papers in Utterson's office yesterday, my cheek muscles are sore from smiling. The future New Hope Mission is almost a reality.

I am not as optimistic that dreadful inspector will stop harassing Henry. Only Doctor Jekyll and I know the truth about Hyde and Jack the Ripper. We need days to turn into months for Newcomen and the world to move on to the next tragedy.

My thoughts return to my idea percolating like coffee on a stovetop. Can New Hope be an oasis for both the women and babies abandoned to the streets of Whitechapel? Louise was the first woman rescued; Lucy, the first baby. Can the bakery make a difference for the ladies and provide money for the babies? One thing is for sure; I will talk at length with both Henry and Louise before we decide to section off a space for a nursery. Can I be sure that baking treats and helping with babies in a communal setting will speed up the ladies' return to sobriety while assuring a safe place to foster the babies? I haven't worked out all the details, but on this sunny and brisk day anything seems possible.

A wet nurse at the Burrough house mentioned to Alice that her sister was a wet nurse there during the summer. Mary McCreary had received their names as dawn arrived, and in no time Paddy provided me with their address at 3 Sheppherd Street. I turn off Commercial Street, and the bustle of carts and carriages fade behind me. The three-story tenement, connected to identical dwellings on either side, is not marked, but the ones on both sides are. As I mount the steps, I am greeted by a child dashing out the front entrance right into me. He was looking at the steps and not where he was going. He is startled when I place my hands on his shoulders. "Might you tell me where I can find Betsy Dyer?"

"Second floor in the back." He uses his left hand to signal which side and spins out of my grasp. "Don't tell her it was me," he says over his shoulder. He sprints to the main thoroughfare whence I came and is gone in a flash. He reminds me of the boys running on Youghal Beach in County Cork. All elbows and knees going full tilt.

Where there are wet nurses, there are babies. I spy two women sitting at the kitchen table from the open front door. A toddler sits on the floor between them, playing with a cloth dolly. The women are having tea. One spots me at the door and puts her index finger to her lips and motions me in. In the top drawer of the dresser next to her is a make-shift crib. As I get closer, I see the child is sleeping.

"And who might ye be?" the other woman asks.

"Mrs. Edward Blackwell. I am hoping to have a word with Betsy Dyer," I whisper.

She looks at the woman who warned me. I address her. "My name is Caroline. We are considering adopting a boy from Mrs. Burrough. Edward thinks I am being overly suspicious, but I am sure something is amiss."

Both women exchange glances. "How did you find us?" The other woman asks.

The lie slides off my tongue like dew on a morning glory. "Dottie Jones told me your name. She quit working for Mrs. Burrough and was more than happy to help me. I stopped at some stores nearby. They set me straight here. It wasn't hard, really."

"Dottie, you say." The other woman eyes me.

I point at both my arms up to my elbows. "Dottie, the laun-dress for Mrs. Burroughs until two days ago."

Both nod at the description.

"We didn't leave that house without money in our pockets, thank you very much. For every boy who suckles, we receive six pence. They are a thirsty bunch," Betsy says.

"Why not any of the girls?" I ask.

"Mrs. Burrough didn't think any of the girls would get adopted." Janine adds.

"I am afraid to query you on this one question. Did any of the mothers return within the year for their babies?" I ask. I think of Rosie somewhere out in the Atlantic Ocean heading for America.

"They would sooner retrieve a family heirloom from a pawnbroker than come back for their own flesh and blood," Betsy says.

"A mother gave Mrs. Burrough her infant boy before sailing to America. My husband and I saw the empty crib. Now you understand why I am concerned," I say. I did see the crib where Baby James lay. "Betsy, were you there when the baby was brought in?"

"The day after. The boys' daytime nurse told me the boy went missing during the night."

"And?"

"Nobody knows who took the baby, and Mrs. Burrough isn't talking," Betsy says.

"The police have been round asking questions, but they aren't asking the right person," Betsy says.

"Who might that be?" I ask.

She tells me, and she describes the policeman. Constable Clarence Collier is on the case.

———

I AM UPSTAIRS above Mary McCreary's store. I dash off a note for Alice and hand it to Paddy along with a couple of shillings. The boy will need a new pair of shoes the way Alice and I are running him back and forth. It's time for us to find out why Alice replaced the girl's nighttime nurse at the foundling house. It is strange that Dottie quit, and the other girl was fired after the baby went missing. I don't know if there is a connection.

We are to meet Seamus here at three o'clock. It's better he hears everything from Mary and me. I don't want him to know about Alice. I will mention Constable Collier in the broadest terms.

"Hope Rosie doesn't get seasick," Mary says.

"Is she going by steamer or sail?" I ask.

"Sail, it's half the cost," Mary replies.

Mary shakes her head. "We are doing all this work for her baby."

"That's right," I say. "We are doing it for the baby and because…" The thought trails off as I need to hear it from Mary.

"Because we can find out what happened to her baby," she says.

"Whether we hand Baby James to Seamus with a soiled nappie or I care for him me self, is not as important as finding the baby," I admit. There, I say it out loud. There is a mystery to solve, and Mary McCreary and I are up for the challenge. I care little about my former sister-in-law. She is off to find a new life in America. She turned too many people against her in London. Better for her to have a fresh start. No need for a new husband to find out about a baby back in the old country. None of us will miss her, including her brother. Mary and I talk about what I have discovered. Mary has had a devil of a time finding any women willing to talk about the foundling house. Giving a baby up is hard and made harder if the mother is not betrothed.

We walk out onto the street. The sun is low, glinting off of standing pools of water. The fresh air is cooling, and the breeze is picking up.

Seamus in the daylight turns heads of the ladies as he makes his way towards us. My pulse quickens as I know it is me he is searching for. Let the women gossip about the lighterman and the do-gooder for now.

He tips his hat. "Francine, Mrs. McCreary."

"We haven't heard from Rosie, so we figured she set sail for America," Mary says.

"Ay. I kissed her goodbye and waved her off."

"Goodbyes are hard." I say, realizing his entire immediate family is dead or just sailed away. He has aunts and cousins but no one to share Sunday dinner with. "Do you think the O'Sullivans will lay claim to Baby James when we find your nephew?"

He shakes his head. "They are adamant that it was not Jimmie who sired the baby."

"And you?" Mary asks.

Seamus is perplexed by the question. "How's that?"

"When we find your nephew, we will bring him to you then," Mary says.

Seamus knows how to take a blow from an angry man or a drunk, but that statement about bowls him over. He staggers back two steps and bobs his head back and forth trying to clear his mind.

"What did you expect us to do?" It is more of a demand than a question from Mary.

"Return the baby from where it was taken until Rosie comes back like she sez."

"Do you really believe she will come back for the baby?" Mary asks.

"Are ye callin' me sister a liar?" Seamus challenges Mary but keeps his temper.

"Maybe she gets settled with a new life and a new husband in America and she has it good there, is all I'm sayin'. No need putting words in me mouth I didn't speak," Mary says.

"Baby can't go back there if we find him, Seamus. You know that. You are the baby's nearest kin; what do you want to do?" I say. Mary and I didn't plan to gang up on Seamus. Are we working for Rosie, who may or may not come back to claim her child? Am I trying to show Seamus I am good enough for his respect?

"I'll tell you that answer when you put him in my arms. So, tell me what you have found out."

"Why must we answer to you if you won't tell us your true intentions?" Mary asks.

"Because when I write her, I can tell her about what you are doing to find her child?"

"It's easier for you to believe Rosie will return? Who will care for her infant and watch him grow until then? He can't go back to that house. I can tell you that much," I say.

"Are you going back on your word, Francine?" Seamus is on a bad footing and doesn't enjoy being on equal footing with two strong women. He tries to remind me who was the boss in our marriage by trying to take control of this meeting.

I step forward between him and Mary and say quietly, only for him to hear, "Come back when you decide what to do when we find the baby, and we will give you our letter to post to Rosie of what we learn." I step back next to Mary. We both fold our arms.

We watch him turn on his heel in a huff and almost collide with Dottie. I whisper to Mary, "I doubt we will see him again."

20

"Whatever did you say to that man? My, is he angry," Dottie says. She is dressed in a clean brown coat over a long woolen dress of the same color. Her face is scrubbed, and her hair is washed and pinned back.

"Hello, Dottie, thank you for meeting me. This is my friend Mary McCreary." Truth be told, Mary is my truest friend and saviour. "She is helping me locate Mrs. Burrough's former employees. She lives here and knows many families."

Dottie nods to Mary, who returns the gesture.

I extract the letter of recommendation and the names of the West End housekeepers in need of a laundress and hold them just out of Dottie's reach. "Do you have the names I am looking for?"

"Just before I stopped working for Mrs. Burrough, she fired the girls' overnight nurse."

I say, "I have been told her first name is Celeste."

Dottie's eyes widened in surprise.

"Do you know her last name?" I ask.

"Pirie—a Scottish lassie." Dottie answers.

"Tell me about her," I ask.

"Red hair like yours, excitable, thin, younger than you."

"How long did she work there?"

"A year maybe more. Not sure. She had a boyfriend waiting for her on Sunday mornings. Archie, I believe—his only day off, so he said.

Mary asked, "Do you know where she lives?"

"Never had a reason to ask? I was there to wash soiled nappies, bedclothes and sheets, not to chat. He's the reason she got fired, I understand."

We wait for her to finish. She looks at the parchment paper I hold by my side. I select the letter of reference but retain the names of prospective employers. "Edward Blackwell exalts you," I say as I hand the reference over to her.

She reads it carefully while the sun dips behind Mary's building. She smiles at the nice things Henry wrote about the woman he never met.

"The night nurse for the boys told me Celeste would unlock the back door in the wee hours of the morning and he'd come up the back stairs to keep her company." Dottie gave a knowing smile to Mary and me.

"The back stairs next to the crib where the baby boy went missing," I said.

"How do you know about that?" she asked.

"Don't you think that information would have been helpful to me, Dottie, in my decision about doing business with Mrs. Burrough?" I give her a stern look.

"Mrs. Burrough found out about Archie's visits from the boys' night nurse after the child went missing." Dottie said. "That's why she fired her."

"You think Archie and Celeste had something to do with the child's disappearance?" Mary asked.

I stood facing both women. "Enterprising Archie and scheming Celeste hatched a plan, wouldn't they know they'd get caught?"

"Not if nobody was aware of them meeting secretly on the third floor," Dottie opined. "Mrs. Burrough was in the business of buying and selling babies, how hard is it for them two to see the same opportunity? Just grab the one closest to the stairs and run down the stairs and out the back door."

"You think so?" Mary asked.

"Celeste, no, Archie, maybe, from the few times I saw him. Did he know a couple having a hard time makin' a baby and for a few quid he could help them out?" She shrugged.

Suddenly, getting the names of other wet nurses didn't seem as important. Find Celeste and Archie and find out who they sold Baby James to. Something else bothers me, but I can't quite put my finger on it. I say, "The woman who gave the missing baby to Mrs. Burrough was short the fee for boarding the baby for the year. She came back the next day with more money and found out her baby was missing. Why didn't Mrs. Burrough know the boy was missing before the woman returned?"

"What if she didn't come back?" Mary asked. We looked at Dottie for an answer.

None was forthcoming. I say, "My darling husband made it clear to Mrs. Burrough he would not wait in line for a baby boy. Do you think Mrs. Burrough had a couple like Edward and I who wanted to skip to the front of the queue? Maybe she didn't have a mother willing to give her baby up for immediate adoption." My thoughts turned immediately to Lucy's mother. Why was the poor girl hurrying after midnight to Mrs. Burrough's house?

Mary says, "Burrough adopts out the new baby boy never expecting Ro, the woman, to return."

December darkness settles on us. The streetlamps are not lit yet. A shiver goes through Dottie, and a chill goes through me, but not from the cold.

Dottie says, "She sells the baby to a buyer in a hurry and then blames it on Celeste."

"I wonder how Mrs. Burrough reacted when she couldn't produce the baby boy for the woman who came back with the last payment?" I say.

"She'd turn to the day nurses and ask what happened?" Mary says.

Absentmindedly, I hand Dottie the names of housekeepers in need of a laundress. She hands me a note with the names of other wet nurses I didn't know about. It was part of the bargain.

Mary is quick to say, "Dottie, if you learn anything else, come here and ask for me. I can get a message to Caroline."

She nods.

I ask, "Would you like me to hail you a cab?"

"I'd rather have the fare and walk, thank you very much," she says.

The practical woman slips my offering of a few coins into a fold in her dress and bids us farewell.

I turn to Mary in the evening's gloaming. "I wonder how Alice can get around to chatting the day nurses up on that question without raising suspicion. On second thought, maybe it's a question for Collier to ask them? How do I reach him now that he is not walking the night beat where the Ripper roamed? Do I leave a message for him at Scotland Yard or where he reports?" Too many questions, too many options. I look at Mary with imploring eyes.

"First ask Alice and then try to meet with the Constable where he does roll call. Does he still owe you a sketch of the girl who died giving birth? You might give him something to work with while we find Celeste Pirie."

I nod on all counts. "What did we get ourselves into, Mary?"

21

———————

I have a plan. Francine, Louise, Utterson and I are not meeting with the architect until half six. This gives me time to see what I can find out. My new partner in New Hope Mission stayed home last evening on account of the torrential rain. She is burning the proverbial candle at both ends with searching for the women in most desperate straits after midnight and trolling the streets by day for women who worked at the foundling house who can give her some clues in the disappearance of Baby James. How our lives have become more complicated since we reclined under the stars on the docks by the Thames nearly a month ago. She learned about Edward Hyde, and we both discovered the true identity of Jack the Ripper that morning. The embers from the red-hot fire of these revelations are still smoldering in both of us.

As I make my way on foot to the Royal College of Physicians on Pall Mall East near Trafalgar Square, I study the coats of arms adorning many of the stately four-story residences. There are depictions of battles with dragons or serpents on some of the family crests. Francine nearly died at the hands of Saucy Jack. I instinctively reach for my letter opener in my left interior coat pocket as I distinguish between the swords and broad-axes carved in archways and above solid wooden doors displaying heavy brass knobs. I am glad to keep my dagger with me now at all times.

After the heat of battle cooled on that memorable night, like the dew settling on the pylons and wharves jutting into the river, we counted two personages vanquished and one man dead. A body needed to be disposed of, and she and I drew closer together, sending it to a watery grave. When that day dawned, I withheld no other secrets from her, and she could finally trust me.

Our goal of forging the New Hope Mission would be losing steam if not for the steely resolve of Louise Anderson. Francine, by her own admission, is being pulled toward caring for babies. One brings joy and happiness to our hearts. Lucy is a miracle baby. Finding her next of kin and the reason her birth mother was desperately seeking the Burrough house occupies much of Francine's thinking. 'Our Lucy' is how we refer to her. Can we adopt her? Can Utterson find a way for Henry Jekyll and Francine Murphy, a married woman, to adopt the child? She and I have discussed such legal banalities while our own relationship remains unclear as the fog rolling over Whitechapel this time of year.

The fate of the Baby James doesn't look promising, but here we are trying to find the boy while his mother has her eyes set on America. I try not to imagine Francine helping her husband in order to get in his good graces. She has nothing to prove to the man who threw her out in the street like a bucket of soapy water. Where was his compassion after she miscarried their baby? Where was the womanly compassion from his sister, who lived under their roof when Francine lay exhausted with a still-born? Francine may be the strongest woman I know, braving the streets night after night in search of the most unfortunate women of Whitechapel. Working and saving to put a roof over their heads and a meager meal on the table as they withdraw from the devil's drink. Tireless time and focus on rescuing them from the most terrible trading of their bodies for gin. I see the results of her efforts and those of Louise Anderson as the women begin their forward journey. They need not look back at the Sodom and Gomorrah of their lives, and neither does Francine. She can start a new family with me; that is, if I am not too old for her and unstable. I want to hold her in my arms the way she held me that morning on the docks. Hyde might want to take things further, and banishing those thoughts have become harder for me. She is a beautiful woman, and she stirs feelings I never knew I had. I am committed to her vision, and if she needs me to help her puzzle out what happened to Baby James, I will. I am doing this for her. Rosie O'Sullivan and Seamus Murphy be damned!

Munk's Roll, which is a relatively new listing of physicians or employees of the College, may help me find the doctor with the bad leg from India, who visits the foundling house regularly. I have a distinctive description. I hope to secure an address for him at the college.

22

"Thank you for your concern, Francine. I am doing fine." Irene says.

She is pretty. Gin hasn't ravaged her looks yet. Her clothes are clean. She must have steady lodging. She is new to the streets, but the signs are there. I am checking in with her around midnight. Misty, thick fog has not dampened the spirits of men looking for their pleasure. She has been doing a brisk business since she arrived in Whitechapel—commanding top payment.

"How so?" I ask.

"Rooms are paid up through to the new year. Plenty to eat where I am boarding. Indoor plumbing, too. Living in luxury, if you ask me."

Hard to think we are almost into 1889. Not so hard to remember I was almost on the street with six women in tow just a few months earlier. Henry and Louise came to our rescue.

"Yet here you are." I wave around the intersection of Whitechapel's busiest streets.

"Make more with one punter than the girls do in a factory on a fourteen-hour shift working their fingers to the bone."

"And they pay for your drinks too, Irene?"

She gives me a cross look. "What are you getting at?"

Sally changes arms with her basket. She points to two haggard, gin-soaked prostitutes pulling desperately at the same man. "You are not like them, Irene. They are a slave to the devil's drink. They will sleep rough tonight rather than miss their last drink for the night. They were pretty once, and lived in nice flats, just remember that." Sally is happy to get the last word in, leaving Irene to stare at the clawing, cawing pair, too young to be old crones.

We walk across the street and stand in the garish lighting of yet another gin palace along Commercial Street and survey the intersection from this different angle when we spot Constable Clarence Collier, but he is not in uniform. Wearing his Sunday best on this awful night tells me he took up Inspector Abberline's advice. I know he is not here to sample Whitechapel's women of the night, or Sally's scones for that matter.

"Constable Collier, why aren't you home in a nice warm bed?" I smile.

"Received this today, and I wanted to hand it to you personally, Mrs. Murphy. Be careful with it," he says. "Abberline gives his regards."

I sense my inspector friend smoothed things over for Collier and convinced him to look into both matters concerning the foundling house while Scotland Yard is stretched too thin chasing down leads on the Ripper.

"You look very proper and businesslike in your attire, Constable Collier," Sally says.

I angle the sketch so the three of us can inspect it under the harsh lighting. Sally and I both nod. The artist captured the unidentified girl's likeness but also her sadness. All three of us saw her in death's repose only a short walk down an alley from here. "Thank you, Clarence," I say. "I will make sure this gets into the right hands to show around the ferry ports."

He tips his hat and is about to return to that warm bed when I ask, "Have you encountered Celeste Pirie or her boyfriend Archie in your investigation of the missing baby?"

"The names are strange to me," he says.

"Until a few days after the boy's disappearance, Pirie was the nighttime girls' nurse on the third floor. Seems Archie would visit her at the foundling house when everybody was sleeping. Something about her leaving the back door open for him after midnight."

He nods.

"Burrough fired her. I have my feelers out to find her. I want you to be there if I do. How would I get a message to you?"

He doesn't object to my efforts to find Celeste Pirie and says, "Abberline. I report to him every morning before I begin my work. My Sargeant has approved this temporary loan to the Yard."

I can hear the pride in his voice. "Do you wonder how Mrs. Burrough acted when Rosie O'Sullivan returned with the last portion of her payment and Rosie wanted to see her baby one last time before sailing off to America?"

I see the confusion on his face. "Was she truly surprised or just acting surprised when they found the crib empty?"

He scratches his chin in thought and says, "The daytime nurses would know how she acted and what she said."

"Both still work there as far as I know," I say.

"Might have a talk with them tomorrow evening when I leave work," he says.

It's my turn to nod.

He looks over my shoulder and says to me quietly, "There is a man heading straight towards you. He doesn't look happy."

I whirl around as Clarence steps next to me. He clenches both fists. Seamus Murphy is glaring at the plainclothesman.

"And who may ye be?" Seamus snarls.

"Whose asking?" Clarence responds with a steely stare.

"I'm her husband." Seamus jabs a finger towards me. While true, he didn't act this way when he tossed me out on my ear back in '86.

"Constable Clarence Collier. Conducting police business."

I touch Clarence's arm. "He's Rosie O'Sullivan's brother." Looking at Seamus. "Constable Collier is looking into the disappearance of Baby James and another matter at the Burrough house. He came out after midnight to find me about the other matter. What brings you to Whitechapel this foggy night?"

What is it about men having to keep staring at each other when it's no longer necessary?

"When youse find Rosie's baby, he will need a proper home. Like you said, he can't go back to the lady who lost him," Seamus says.

Both Sarah and Clarence step closer. What an interesting group we make. No one drinking, no one making lewd overtures. Money and sex are not being discussed.

We wait for Seamus to tell us the reason for his second sojourn onto these sin-filled streets. He balks and stutters, "My lips to your ears only, Francine."

There was a time when he nibbled on my ear and cooed sweet nothings when we recovered from our lovemaking. A heat rises in my privates. My mind may have stamped out memories of happier times with Seamus, but my body hasn't. Even with Rosie snoring in the other room, we found ways to quake and quiver without rousing her. I shake my head at him, but say to Clarence, "A moment."

Seamus and I repair to a darker corner of the street, and I let my irritation slip. "I was in the middle of asking the good constable to do important interviews at the Burrough house. His authority in an official investigation carries more weight than anything I could accomplish."

"I took counsel from what you said, Francine. When did you become so…?"

"Smart," I say with anger.

"Fierce is the word I was searching for."

I take it as a compliment, and it diffuses some of my anger.

"Fending for myself on these streets has taught me much, Seamus."

"I can see that."

"Well, I don't want to keep the constable waiting on the matter you first brought to me on these very streets. What is it?"

"I work in the daytime, and you work in the nighttime, I can care for the baby while you are away, and you can do the same while I am working."

"You live on Rosemary Lane, and I live at Cavendish Square. How do you propose we pass the baby back and forth?"

He looks as puzzled by my response as I am with his plan.

"No, Francine, if you find the baby, we give it a proper home."

"What?" I sputter.

"You said out loud what I was dreading. Rosie is not coming back for the baby. If you find it alive, I am his kin. What is it to say we can't raise him as our own?

"Are you daft?" I ask.

"You called me worse names and acted crazy. You gave me no choice to ask you to leave. I will put that aside for the sake of Rosie's child. I am asking you to return."

A stubborn man is letting his guard down in front of a woman who hurt him badly. I always assumed I said and did some horrible things to cause him to throw me out of my home. He will put that all aside for the sake of the baby. Maybe there is more to it. Maybe he wants to know the Francine Murphy I've become.

"When I woke up from my one and only blackout from

drinking, I found myself with Mary McCreary telling me why I woke up in her flat. I lost my baby, I lost my mind, and when I came out of it, I had no home to return, no husband to console me, my clothes thrown into a burlap bag. You want me to return now with no discussion for over almost three years?"

"Blackout?" he asks. "No one told me."

"What if we don't find the baby or worse? What then? No baby, then no deal? It sounds like you would be happy to go on living the way you are now without your sister weighing you down like an anchor."

"You said and did those things while you were in a blackout? I didn't know." Seamus gave me a vacant stare. He is ciphering the sums of our lives since then, and things are slowly adding up. He looks upward and not where he walks as he turns and leaves me standing in the shadows.

Sally gives me a puzzled look. Clarence's gaze follows Seamus as he disappears into the fog.

23

I knock on the door connecting my room to Henry's. Lucky is circling my legs and thinks he is getting some of the warm cranberry scone I am bringing his rescuer. We've made this a habit when I return from Whitechapel. We talk about my nocturnal travels, Lucy, plans for New Hope and his efforts toward finding Baby James and the identity of Lucy's mother.

He is wearing the same clothes of a West End gentleman as when he sent me off in a cab hours earlier. "Was it this foggy in Whitechapel?" he asks as we take our usual spots by the window overlooking the garden. Our knees almost touch, and our dog is an easy reach between us.

"Worse."

He nods, chews blissfully on the scone and pets Lucky. He slips Lucky a pig's ear, and our little dog settles in for a serious chew.

"I can't lose patience with the women. They will come to me when they are ready. None took our invitation to ride with us tonight to a warm house, bed, breakfast and bath. The drink has a powerful hold on them. Maybe if we get an early winter, we might see some interest." I add. I tell him how I planted a few ideas with Constable Collier and then I unroll the sketch. He never saw Lucy's mother in the flesh.

"She looks so sad," he says.

"Dying in an alley on a heap of rags and newspapers with no one to care for her in her time of need." He holds a corner of the sketch. I hold the other. Our cheeks are almost touching as we angle the thick drawing parchment to better catch the lamplight from his bedstand. "I think she yelled out not from the pain of giving birth but to get someone's attention for her baby," I say. "Her last act on earth was to cry out for passersby to have mercy on her newborn." We set it down on sideboard.

"If it wasn't you caring for the ladies. If you didn't stop to talk to Alice who in a previous life cared for infants," he says.

I jump aboard his train of thought. "If Sally's mother didn't teach Sally how to bake, we might not have had a reason to tarry with Alice for as long as we did. Alice knew what to do."

"Divine intervention?" he asks.

"If Hyde wasn't there when the Ripper had his hands around my throat," I say.

"There are many things science, medicine and religion do not have answers for," he says.

"We can agree on miracles."

He bobs his head back and forth in mild agreement.

"Lucy is a miracle." I say.

"Finding your sister-in-law's baby alive will be a miracle," he says.

"Just after midnight, her brother found me talking with Collier; he acted jealous," I say.

Henry stiffens when I mention Seamus. Lucky notices his reaction as well, and he stops working on his treat.

"If we find Baby James, he agrees to care for him at night when I am in Whitechapel. He asks me to care for the little one when he goes to work."

Henry tries to puzzle the arrangements out. "How..."

"I know," I say. "I was wondering just how it would work out and that is when he said we should care for the baby together in the home where I was no longer welcome."

His hands tremble as he pets Lucky. "What did you say to that?"

"We never got that far. The eejit did not know until today I was in a bloody blackout when I raged at him. Only he knows what I said or how I acted. I have always suspected the worst. He never mentioned a word to Rosie or Mary McCreary as far as I know." I've never used coarse language in all my dealings with Doctor Jekyll. Mary has taught me a few other words that would make a nun blush, but he needs to understand the importance of what happened over two years ago. "Seamus believed I was in my sane mind when I lashed out at him. How could he not understand that losing a baby, falling into deep despair and drinking an entire bottle of whiskey might make me act strangely?"

"Did you ever tell him you blacked out and had no memory of what you said or what you did?"

"Not until tonight."

"Did Mary or anybody else intercede on your behalf with Seamus when you came to your senses?"

"No."

"Francine, did you ever think you might have only told him the truth of how he was not there for you when you needed him the most, that a husband needed to assure his wife everything would be alright, that together they would mourn the loss of their child, and he would be strong for you when you most needed him."

I avert my eyes from his. Henry is making a promise to me while pointing out Seamus did none of those things.

He brushes the imaginary crumbs from his vest before adding. "You might have pointed out he didn't have the courage to place you first in his life and that his sister should have acted like a guest in your home, that if she could not be respectful of your marriage, she should find her own place to live? Maybe it was not you screaming or acting like a lunatic; maybe you spoke your truth, and he could not face the truth of being awful to you. His pride would not allow him to be talked to that way."

I feel faint and flushed at the same time. For a man who was emotionally stifled with all his feelings bottled up inside, he sure has picked a good time to shed those shackles.

He continued. "If those were not the words you spoke to him after losing your baby, maybe those are the words he needs to hear now. Maybe there is a reason Mary McCreary didn't want you to look back, only to look forward, like you teach the ladies here."

Lucky is too entranced by Henry's soothing words and light caresses to work on his late-night snack. Henry is applying a feathery touch to my cheeks. He has never been so bold in all our quiet moments. Maybe it's not about him; maybe it's about me and the hurt I buried with my baby. The hurt I tried to dissolve with whiskey, the hurt only made worse by the drink. The hurt Seamus inflicted and refused to heal in me.

Tears form in my eyes. Henry holds my face, closes the distance and gently kisses them away. I sob mightily, and my shoulders quake. The dam is breaking. He brings me in close in a warm, strong, yet gentle embrace. Lucky remains at our feet. Not now, boy.

———

THE LAMPLIGHT FLICKERS in my bedchamber. I hold Francine in my arms. Edward would have me sweep her into my bed. In this moment, she needs me to give her a safe space to heal from the wounds of her heart. She has shown ultimate strength to the women she rescues. I am only returning a pitiful portion. From the day I met her until now, I never saw her waver in her determination about her future. It is her past and a man from her past which tests her resolve. The Francine that was is not the woman I am gently hugging now. A determined and unfailing love showered upon her by Mary McCreary is the love and strength she carries in her mission. The leaky rowboat of a plan offered by her husband, the lighterman, doesn't float for me. But it is not for me to say it aloud.

Her heaving sobs subside, and I hold her shoulder at arm's length. "Do I understand it correctly that returning to your marital abode is predicated upon finding the baby?"

She sniffles and nods.

"Is it true he did not search you out for almost three years until his sister had a problem he thought you could help him and her with?"

She responds in the same way again.

"And that, faced with having to care for the baby himself, only then did he consider you to share his burden?"

Her eyes met mine.

I say, "I will help you find Rosie's baby, and then you can decide what to do. I cannot tell you what to do. In the end, it is your decision. I will respect what you decide. I am schooled in the affairs of the body and what ails it, not so much with affairs of the heart, I'm afraid."

She stands and takes the towel from my washbasin and wipes her eyes. She unpins her luxurious red hair and allows it to fall down over her shoulder to the middle of her back. Lucky is following her moves with a curious tilt of his head. The door between our rooms closes with an almost imperceptible click, thanks to her gentle touch.

Francine dims the lamp and leads me to my bed.

24

The soft, moist tongue in my ear wakes me from my slumber. That Francine would greet me this way after the most wonderful night in my life reassures me it was not a dream. How do I describe the feelings of tender love and ferocious lovemaking from our surprise coupling? I open my eyes and turn my face to greet her. "Good morning, my darling."

Lucky licks my nose.

I sit up instantly and help him to the floor. My clothes are strewn about there. There is no sign of my lover, and the door between our rooms is shut. Standing now, I spot a note on my dresser. *A warm bath awaits you. Dress and join us for breakfast.* I stow it in my billfold; no need for the maid to find it.

Of course I must bathe; the women would pick up the scent of sex on me in a heartbeat. I will let Francine decide how she will greet me upon my arrival at the breakfast table. My father's gold pocket watch and the angle of the December sun through my windows tells me I awoke later than rest of the Jekyll household. The smell of sugary baked goods and cinnamon instantly triggers my hunger.

Throwing on bedclothes, I shuffle barefoot down the hall. I have much planned for this day and mentally prepare where I will go first. The bathwater is perfect. The smell of her perfume permeates the air. I drink it in as I sink into the tub. The business of finding the Indian doctor with the bad leg can wait. I close my eyes and recall sharing intimacy with the red-headed woman of pale skin with exquisite freckles in the most delicious places. I commit to memory every touch and caress from the moment she took me by the hand until our last kiss before drifting off to sleep. I luxuriate in the soapy water until it turns cold.

I towel off with a monogrammed Egyptian cotton towel, shave with a steady hand and retreat to my room to change into a freshly starched shirt and pressed suit. My boots are polished and show no signs of the deposits made on London cobblestones by many of its beasts of burden.

A Twining's black tea blended with bergamot steams next to an exquisite warm muffin with dates. I take my place at the kitchen table. I have eschewed formal dining while the women are under my roof. Lucky takes up his spot under the table, waiting for me to not so accidentally drop a morsel. Sally, Agatha and Jane are preparing baskets to take to the New Hope Bakery food cart in the market. Louise and the others are up to their elbows in flour or are kneading dough. Francine walks in from the pantry holding Lucy with one arm lightly against her chest, where I had nuzzled several hours earlier. She carries a mesh bag of figs in the other hand. The others have their backs turned to us, and she allows her gaze to linger with smiling eyes on me. She turns to Sally. "And where do you want these?"

"Over there," she points to the far end of the table away from me. When Francine sets down the figs, she winks at me and turns with a vivacious swing of her hips.

I ruin the cup of tea with too much cream, but it is worth

not taking my eyes off of her to follow her around the room. I absentmindedly bite into the muffin and onto one of the hardened dates. I come close to breaking a tooth. "Ouch!"

"That was a test muffin, Dr. Jekyll," Sally says. "I should have warned you."

"Delicious," I mumble as I remove the rock hard nugget, glad that it is not part of my lower right molar.

There is a lightness and gaiety in their banter as they go about baking. I watch the flurry of activity. With more baskets filling, the oven emptying and filling, the reverse for the sink with pots and pans. Do they know? I doubt Francine told them. Can the women who practiced depraved sexual acts for money spot a man and woman who enjoyed blissful pleasure amongst them now? When the boys from my boarding school returned from a night of debauchery, it was the ones who didn't brag about their exploits I knew found their needs satiated. Francine and I will keep our secret for now.

Francine sits across from me with a sleeping Lucy snoring lightly. "Remind me of your plans for the day, Henry?" It is the first time she has addressed me thus in front of the ladies. Is this a signal of future good tidings?

"I have a plan to find the doctor who treats the infants at the foundling house. And you?"

"Finding Celeste Pirie and her boyfriend Archie. I would like to hear what they say before Constable Collier questions them."

Looking at Louise Anderson, Francine asks, "Tomorrow is our meeting with the contractors at the Mission; are you able to attend?"

Louise looks around and says, "I think Sally will keep everybody busy until tea."

"There is a matter of how to configure the first-floor rooms I would like to discuss with you both before we travel there," Francine says.

Louise gives us her full attention

"How many women like Rosie O'Sullivan have no family to speak of caring for their babies? What if they cannot depend on kindly neighbors or widows to care for their infants when the women go to find steady work?" Francine asks us.

"I've not a clue," I say

"Can Alice teach our ladies how to care for infants the way Sally is teaching us how to bake?" Francine's plan is becoming apparent. "By taking in babies and young children for a small daily fee and by doing out baking we can generate revenues while providing two valuable skills for the ladies to take with them when they leave New Hope."

"Are you suggesting we add a nursery to the building plans?" I ask.

"When we find Baby James and if we cannot find Lucy's family, we will have two babies to begin with." Francine shifts Lucy to her shoulder.

Before either Louise or I answer, Alice bursts in the back door. She is breathless and distraught.

"The poor girls. I stayed awake all night. Two of them, they… they…"

"What, Alice?" Francine asks. Lucy must sense Francine's concern and wakes from a deep sleep and cries. Alices reaches for Lucy and holds her close.

"The girls, they never fuss. They never cry. All night they sleep. I change them while they sleep. They don't take milk. They never act hungry. All night I hear the boys downstairs. Not a peep from the girls."

"What happened to the two girls, Alice?" Louise asks loudly. Everyone in the kitchen stops baking and gathers at the far end of the table where Alice stands with Lucy next to where Louise, Francine and I are seated.

"They are dead. They never woke up. I could tell something was wrong. As soon as Mrs. Burrough awoke, I told her something was wrong with those two. She sent for the doctor. She told me I could go home and get some sleep, but I was too upset and told her I would wait."

I stood and ushered her into my seat, Alice handed Lucy back to Francine before collapsing in the chair. A cup of tea and some shortbread was placed on the setting before her.

"I kept asking myself what I could have done differently. The day nurse always told me Mrs. Burrough gave the girls something to keep them quiet. Looking at them, I could see they weren't as strong as the boys. It was so unnerving to see them so...so..."

"Drugged. Twenty girls are sedated at night. They eat less and cause no problems," I say.

"Drugged?" Francine asks.

"I didn't understand how not one girl would fuss. Of course, I thought the day nurse gave them something in their milk to calm them, something natural, but not drugs. But it makes sense now that you say it," Alice replies.

"What happened next?" Louise asks.

"When the doctor arrived, he pronounced them dead with only brief examination, and Felicity took both babies downstairs to the parlor, Mrs. Burrough was stern with me and told me to go home and get some sleep and come back tonight."

"So she wasn't upset with you?" Francine asked.

"Why, I did nothing wrong?" Alice asked in a shrill, loud voice.

"Francine is not implying you did anything wrong, Alice. What I surmise is that neither Mrs. Burrough nor the doctor were surprised by their deaths." Before she can fully grasp that answer, I ask, "Was it an Indian fellow with a bad leg?"

The exhaustion from her night worries and the trek here shows on her face. She nods.

"Did you catch his name?"

"I heard the housemaid greet him; however, his name was lengthy, and I didn't catch it."

"How did he arrive?" Francine asks.

"Not by cab, on foot. I suppose, but he wasn't out of breath."

"He's been there before for that exact reason. No need to rush. How many times worries me." I say.

25

"It will be easier to find the Pirie girl. She's Scottish. There are too many Archies," Mary McCreary tells me. We meet across the street from the foundling house. Cloaked by the afternoon shadows on this cold, windy afternoon, we both are stamping our feet and are trying to keep warm. Better not to be seen by Mrs. Burrough. Mary needs to take in the house where a baby disappeared last week and two more died last night.

"Alice is not going back there," I say. We both stare at the brick building bathed in fading sunlight, hoping it will give us some clues. "I'm afraid the shock of seeing those babies sent her over the deep end. She was doing so well. Louise and I are questioning if we allowed her to go out alone too soon."

"Ay, she is different," Mary says. "Breathing life into Lucy and not showing any of the signs of the withdrawal fooled you. Thank your lucky stars she came straight to you with the news and didn't go off on a drinking binge."

"She's a wreck and inconsolable, but you are right; we are lucky." Carts and cabs cross in front of us. Even in this part of Whitechapel, business still carries on when something evil is in the air.

I take her hand in mine. It is calloused and cold. I say, "Did you ever find out what I said or did to Seamus to end my marriage?"

"Where does that come from? What's past is past. Look at you now, Francine. Look at you now."

"Well." I start slowly. "Seamus sought me out on the street the other night and made a proposal about Baby James." Mary arches an eyebrow.

"He said if we find the boy, he will care for him while I go about my New Hope business and I would care for the child while he plies the river trade."

Mary is good at ciphering, and what I told her doesn't add up.

"I know, I know; that is what I wondered as well. Mr. Murphy proposed we take up house together and treat the child as our own."

"I hope you didn't agree to do that," she says.

I've had some strange ideas since she took me under her wing, so I am accustomed to her questioning my sanity. "Which brings me back to my original question, Mary. He said he would forgive me for what I said and did for the sake of the child, but he never told me the truth of why he sent me away."

"Bit and pieces, and it doesn't matter anymore. It really doesn't. How does that change anything?" Mary takes my hand in both of hers. I asked, and she answered with a stubborn defiance I've learned not to question.

"He was shocked to find out I woke up from a three-day blackout and I had no recollection of what I said or did."

"I didn't tell him anything about your blackout. He threw you out when you needed him the most. I've not had a word with him until Rosie gave away her child."

Interesting way of looking at Rosie's actions. "Henry, Doctor Jekyll," I corrected myself, "asked if all I did was point out to my husband that he let me down and allowed his sister to run all over us. I didn't need to do anything outrageous to trigger Seamus to send me packing."

"That's more or less what I remember," Mary says. She has her reasons to be elusive on this topic, and I do not push back.

"Being blackout drunk didn't take away from the fact I miscarried and was beside myself in grief. Seamus should have understood that, Henry said."

"Dr. Jekyll is a good man, Francine."

"Good enough for me, Mary?"

"Oh, definitely."

Between Seamus and Henry, there have been no other men in my life. Getting sober and using what Mary McCreary taught me with the ladies in New Hope gave me a focus like a magnifying glass with the sun's rays. When I have those womanly feelings, those physical needs, I quickly return my thoughts to what my mission is.

Last night, Henry made me realize he could hold his feelings for me in check if I returned to my lawfully wedded husband. I realized he would still love me for who I am. But he also made me feel loved with no expectations to return his affection. Yes, the distinguished West End gentleman, who is twice my age, displayed courage when faced with emotional hurt. His experience and emotional travails have given him an insight into the human heart, and I realized we could explore our carnal desires from a place of mutual respect and, dare I say, love. "I think so too. Last night, our partnership took on a new meaning. I realized how much he loves me, and Seamus only acts like I would no longer be an inconvenience to have around. Could Seamus learn to love me again?"

"I doubt it," Mary interrupts my musings. "How long before he demands you return to the girl he married, not the woman you are? Could you accept that?"

"No."

"But your doctor accepts you for who you are and would do anything for you with no strings attached."

I smile. "If I waited for the proper gentleman to act on his feelings, he might feel he was taking advantage of our situation. I am glad I took him to bed."

"What took you so long, dearie?" Mary hugs me.

"So, you knew he was good for me, why didn't you say anything?"

"I cannot offer my thoughts on the affairs of the heart. I can only advise you to become the woman you were always meant to be. I never said and nor would I now tell you to return to your husband. You have the means to divorce him, Francine."

"But in the eyes of the church?" I say.

"The women you rescue—what does the church say about them? How would any of them be treated if they slipped in the side door during Sunday morning services after walking the streets all night? What would the ushers do? What about Lucy or Lucy's mother when she was alive? How would they respond to an unwed mother in need? Tell me about the church in your experience? How did they help you when you buried your child? Where were they when Seamus threw you out on your ear? You are helping women and babies in need. You have a benefactor who loves you. Move forward knowing you are worthy of your achievements, but mostly, move forward knowing you are loved. There are only two questions that remain."

The sun peeks between buildings and we are bathed in light. Mary shields me from any eyes peering out of the Burrough house.

"What's that?" I ask.

"It's not what you did or said to Seamus back then; it is how the men in your life treat you now."

"And the second."

"When will you love yourself for who you are? I know you

should tell the ladies to see who they will become in the future. The present is too close to their past. They need to look outward into the future and envision brighter days. When they do graduate from New Hope Mission, they will see themselves as who they are and where they want to go. Why can't you do the same for yourself? Why can't you forgive yourself? This is your last step, Francine."

Our tears glisten on the cobblestones of Whitechapel.

26

"Good afternoon, Doctor Jekyll. There have been no sightings of Jack the Ripper, nor Edward Hyde since the night I encountered Hyde in Whitechapel," Newcomen says. "Do you find that strange?" He cuts out in front of me with a constable tagging behind. We are of equal height, and his breath needs a mint. His carriage must have followed my carriage from the West End to Whitechapel, and he waited until I exited this chemist shop. I am betting the bad-legged doctor is getting his drugs locally near the Burrough house, and I am determined to find his whereabouts. My cabbie has put all the local chemists on a map expanding outward from the spot where the babies were poisoned. My business is not for the nosey Newcomen, and I must rid myself of him before all the shops close.

I consciously pat my letter opener in my interior coat pocket. Would he remember it if I waved it in front of him? "Not at all, Inspector," I say. "The Ripper waited sometime between two of his killings, and you said yourself Hyde was not seen for the years of my absence from London." I move to my right to get around him, and he blocks my path.

"Mister Hyde told me he had reason to slay Sir Danvers Carew and, like a good policeman, I am looking into it."

"I've not spoken to him since the slaying, Inspector," I say truthfully. I have never spoken to Hyde in my entire life, and one reason had to do with the dead man we are discussing and what that man did to me. Hyde has left me with the nightmares and memories of how Carew and my mother sexually assaulted me when my father was away on business.

"Certainly, he must have told his good friend Doctor Jekyll why he harbored such animosity for a man who led an exemplary life."

"It never came up in conversation," I say truthfully again.

"He's a strange bird, that Hyde, so strange, he was never seen in your company, but yet you fronted him significant sums of money."

"Do you have associates or acquaintances your closest friends have never met?" I ask. "I am a doctor, and Hyde was a down on his luck investor. Can you understand why I didn't show him off at the clubs or at social events?"

"He didn't fit in with West End friends?"

"Hardly," I say.

"Yet he confided in you his poor investments and convinced you to front him."

"Yes." That is the story I have stuck to for decades.

"And he never mentioned why he hated Carew so much that, when he encountered him on the street, he beat and stomped him to death?"

"As you said, Inspector, Hyde was a strange bird."

"No, Doctor Jekyll, I said he is a strange bird. You are talking about your associate in the past tense, if I remember my classroom English correctly."

"Very true, Inspector Newcomen, Edward Hyde is dead to me. Now, if you excuse me, I am a doctor and I am looking for drugs." He doesn't need to know why. I wait for him to move.

I've learned the hard way that he always needs to get the last word in.

"I've been to your brother's residence, and I am told he is abroad. Can you tell me when he will return?"

"Soon," I say. "When I see him next, I will tell him you wish to talk to him about Hyde." I think he was expecting a different response. His last question was a signal he held an ace in his hand; little did he know when it comes to my brother, Hyde and Saucy Jack, I hold two of the other three. A grim smile creases my lips.

"I will find Hyde, Doctor Jekyll, and when I do, you will be the first to know."

"Thank you, Inspector."

He motions to the constable who witnessed our exchange, and they roughly brush past on my right side as they step towards their waiting cab.

I remain rooted to that spot until they are out of sight, and then my shoulders heave as I take in gulps of air.

"Everything 'right, Guv?" my driver asks.

"You never want to cross that policeman," I say. "Where is our next stop?" I climb into the cab and plop down in a corner covered in shadow.

I describe the unique doctor to chemist after chemist. I tell them he is treating a child my rather well-off friend is hoping to adopt, and I need to hear firsthand about the infant's health. Holding coins in my hand silently tells them I will pay for the information.

"An Indian, you say?" he shrugs. "Not here, I am sorry."

"He's a bum leg?" A shake of the head from the next chemist.

"An Indian with a bad leg? I would have remembered him if he had come in more than once," the next chemist replied.

The next shop is closed. *Death in the Family* is scrawled on a note on the door.

We make wider and wider arcs around Whitechapel with much of the same confused looks and shakes of their heads.

In the last shop the cabbie is aware of, I make my pitch. "I am looking for an Indian doctor I am told has a bad leg, maybe from military action. Does he come in here?"

The chemist climbs down from his ladder after gently placing a glass container with an amber liquid on the highest shelf. "He was in here two days ago for the usual."

I decide to forget the ruse and make up a new one. I slip the coins into my front pocket out of sight below the counter. "My name is Doctor Jekyll. He treats children at a home where adoptions take place. I am caring for a child from that home and am having trouble diagnosing the illness."

"Is it a baby?"

My pulse quickens, and I am not afraid to show my piqued interest. "Why, yes."

He turns and climbs back up the ladder to retrieve the container with the amber liquid. "My guess is that the baby is showing signs of laudanum withdrawal. This is what he gives them. You need to taper off slowly. The full dose is written on the label."

My hand with the coins automatically slides the money across the counter. "No need to make change, but I would like to talk to him about the cough rattle I am hearing."

"Vijay Meherhomji. Hold on. I have sent medicines to his home for his leg." He reaches into the card carrier behind the counter. He writes it down and hands it to me. "There you are, Doctor. Good luck." The tip is commensurate with the extra service.

I shake the bottle. "He orders much of this?"

"Yes, he tells me he visits many homes with hundreds of children. He comes in often."

I nod. "Yes, of course, that makes sense. Thank you again. If you should see him, mention my name." I give him my card.

I walk out into the setting sun and turn to better read the dosage.

"Everything 'right, Guv?"

This dosage is what I would give a full grown woman. Laudanum is a highly addictive tincture of opium tempered with alcohol.

"Cavendish Square," I mumble, deep in thought. "Whatever my fare is, double it. The value of your knowledge of Whitechapel is immeasurable."

Even the horse feels the driver's happiness as we make haste with the sun setting in glorious purples and magenta, turning gray. No wonder the girls sleep without protest. Even a watered down dose for their age, size, and weight is exactly the extended sleep Alice described to us this morning. Tonight, I will accompany Sally and Francine to Whitechapel. I will wake the doctor and have a chat with him about why he is treating hundreds of infants with laudanum. There are cheaper sedatives, but considering it's ordered in this bulk, I am concerned about why it is Meherhomji's drug of choice. A double dose will cause what Alice experienced with the two girls.

As we clip-clop along, I try to puzzle out how the doctor charges for his work. How many houses like the Burrough house must he visit to eke out a living? Now that I have a name, I can find out what hospitals he has privileges with. That will have to wait until another day.

Newcomen's veiled threats enter my thoughts. He will never find Hyde or my brother for that matter. What concerns me is what tricks he has up his sleeve for me. He assumes I have sheltered Hyde from him, and I am to pay for this misdeed.

I put those thoughts aside and try to imagine what is in store for me when Francine and I return exhausted from Whitechapel. Will we share more than a warm scone and our furry friend?

27

Utterson's butler answers the door and looks beyond me to the carriage idling by the gates. The man is younger than Poole, but not by much. My barrister takes good care of him. Even at the dinner hour, his attire is impeccable, and his shoes sparkle in the lamplight.

"Is he home?" I ask.

"Was he expecting you, Doctor Jekyll? He didn't ask me to have the cook set another place setting."

"I've some nasty business to report."

"Please come in," he says.

I half-turn to the cabbie and wave my hat.

"G'evening, Guv," he bids me adieu. I changed my mind about going home. The distance to my lawyer's from the bowels of Whitechapel was closer than Cavendish Square. He has my generous tip and now can take fares from those going to West End shows.

Utterson is a friend and confidant, although I never told him about my true relationship with Edward Hyde. When Hyde was running roughshod around the West End and Soho after murdering Carew, I never told him I had a plan to rid Hyde of my life. Two years later, when I returned tan and fit from my hiatus in the West Endies, he never questioned me. Without having said a word to him, he took care of my affairs. Everything was as it should be upon my return.

He pushes his evening's beverage away and stands to greet me. "Jekyll."

"Thank you for seeing me this evening," I say.

"Have you eaten?"

His plate of food with its comforting aroma beckons me to be truthful. "Famished."

He looks over my shoulder. "The same for good doctor and one more of these." He points to his glass of wine.

I hear doors close behind me. Never one to pry, he waits for me to tell him the nature of my business.

"The brutish Newcomen and one of his minions followed me from the West End to a chemist's shop in Whitechapel."

"You are an accomplished chemist, Henry, what was your need to go there for a remedy?"

"That is the second matter I want to discuss with you."

I look at remaining roll on the bread plate.

"Help yourself. Not as good as what your ladies bake, but if one's hungry…"

I reach for it, slice it in half, lather both warm sides with creamy butter, and before they disappear, I say, "There's something else I should mention as well."

He smiles. "Newcomen is the main course, the chemist for dessert and the last matter with brandy and a good Cuban."

As I chew and wash it with a gulp of wine, he adds, "Your shipping agent has had no luck on this side of the Channel with the sketches. He has taken to this task like your dog with a bone. He is sure the answer is on the continent."

Roast beef dripping in gravy with mashed potatoes and peas is placed in front of me. It vies for my attention with what my dining partner is about to say. "Allow me a bite first so I can give you my undivided attention."

I close my eyes to savor the meat—reminds me of better days when my brother visited for Sunday dinner after all his visits with the congregation.

———

WE ARE two women in the worst section of the worse part of London. No amount of cajoling on my part and swearing on Mary McCreary's part convinces a cab driver to pick us up. We walk briskly as much to keep warm and to avoid unwanted attention from robbers and thieves. We wonder how far Celeste Pirie traveled to go to the Burrough house. She would be going by cab or on foot at this same hour. In the summer, plenty of daylight, the second week of December, plenty of darkness and danger.

"Burrough is English and Pirie is Scottish," Mary says between chattering teeth.

"The wet nurses and laundresses are English too."

"Irish need not apply," she says.

It's a common refrain since the potato famine, when hordes of starving Irish crossed the sea in search of work and food. "Even a woman as desperate as Burrough has her beliefs. Can't change them," I say.

Mary laughs, "It's a good thing Alice failed to mention her most recent form of self-employment."

"We sent a note from Cavendish Square; Alice found a new employer and wouldn't be returning tonight. The real reason is knowing two babies died under her supervision."

"Something tells me they were just the cost of doing business," Mary says. "I hope never to see that house again. I've a bad feeling about that place. Make sure all your ladies have time away from the streets and the drink before they venture out on their own. Promise me, Francine."

"Yes, we are lucky, and as usual, you are right."

"Finding Pirie, who goes out with an Archie, won't be easy," she says.

"They have to eat, and they have to worship. First thing tomorrow, I will visit the stores and churches within walking distance around that wretched house," I say.

McCreary's is closed when we arrive, but Gabby has stew on the stove, bread warming in the oven and hot tea at the ready. Both Mary and I wash the Burrough house from our hands and face. It's not the first time I felt that way. Not a spiritualist, nor one who thinks much about the afterlife, I know what I feel about that location. I silently curse Rosie for bringing her child there and for an infinitesimal moment regret telling her we would find Baby James. Mary and I thank Gabby for keeping the stew warm, and we devour it.

———

UTTERSON and I adjourn to the library. We sink into amply cushioned deep brown leather chairs angled towards a roaring fire in the massive brick and stone fireplace. We have refilled our snifters twice already, and our stogies are not much longer for this world. We use them to make our points with exclamation. Relaxed and not in the least intoxicated, I will relight my cigar for the walk home to mask the smell of alcohol on my breath. I have been chastised once by Francine about being drunk where the ladies lived, and I have not repeated that mistake. The scar on my right forearm tingles when I think of how I almost died that night; my arm shielding my throat from The Ripper's slash. The alcohol I consumed was for medicinal purposes, but she would have nothing to do with my excuses. I almost lost my life and the love of my life that fateful morning when Jack killed two women.

Francine, Sally and I will journey later tonight back to Whitechapel; they on their appointed rounds, and I to awaken an unsuspecting doctor from his slumber with many questions of deep concern. Utterson agreed to my ruse of treating an adopted child from the Burrough house with inexplicable symptoms. This gives me reason to bang on his door. After all, I am desperate for a cure for my well-heeled friends whose child is very sick. One more brandy with my friend, a warm fire to steel me against the chill and a few minutes of quick repose where nothing further needs to be said. The wood crackles and spits cinders at the screen, and that is all that occupies my brain for the time being. As for the other matters, we have formulated plans.

———

MY FEET KNOW the way from Mary McCreary's store to Rosemary Lane. I see a light in the window. Better that I talk to Seamus here than drag him away from his mates at the pub. Mary and I talked about what I needed to do. It was more of Mary listening and me talking, but she didn't interrupt me or call me daft. I repeated my vow twice to her to summon the courage to do what I needed to do. There was a time when whiskey would have given me the courage to speak my mind, but I know where that landed me. Mary took me from the belly of the whale and brought me to the surface. She taught me the drink supplied only false courage, and little by little I believed I could say what was on my mind without worry.

There is to be a reckoning between Seamus and I, between former husband and wife. I need it to take place tonight, before I visit Henry's bed chamber again.

28

The cab dropped Francine and Sally off in front of Ten Bells Pub. Tonight, they are tempting the ladies with apple fritters and cinnamon twists. I am glad I had a sumptuous meal with Utterson and am not craving the sweet treats.

I take in the sky above as we travel to my destination. Fast-moving clouds play hide and seek with the nearly full moon. When I sojourned in the West Indies, I could tell whether it was waxing or waning, but since my return to London, there were months when an entire week of rain and fog made such observations difficult.

The ruse of being a prospective parent looking to adopt an heir and now acting as a doctor frantic for a cure will catch up with me at some point. I want to make sure my conversation goes past the girl and brings me to the whereabouts of Rosie O'Sullivan's boy. Lying is a personality defect I am trying to correct since I longer have to account for Mister Hyde. There is no lying to Francine. I almost lost her twice from prefabrications surrounding Edward.

I arrive at the address supplied by the chemist for the bad-legged Indian doctor. Why didn't I think of coming here first?

The ramshackle wooden building is three stories, with a market selling spices and delicacies from India taking up the entire first floor. All the shopkeeper needed to do was point upstairs. The separate staircase on the left side of the store is locked. As I contemplate what to do next, the door flies open, and a man steps out. He is Indian and walks with a normal gait. I rush to the door before it closes. He turns and eyes me warily.

I smile, point upstairs and say, "I am bringing remedies for Doctor Meherhomji. He must have fallen asleep before unlocking the door. Thank you."

He nods at me. I gave him a known name and a reasonable excuse to be lurking by the entrance there after midnight. When did this respectable London physician become such a bold face liar?

The flat is on the third floor and at the rear. It is quiet in the hallway; hints of Indian cooking emanate from behind the ill-fitting doors of the other flats I pass to reach his door. There is no name, no other means of identifying him. I am sure he caters to the Indian population in this densely populated section of Whitechapel, as evidenced by the well-worn carpet leading to his door.

I knock and take a deep breath. Tonight I am a frantic doctor of a newly adopted girl from the Burrough house, and I am troubled by what I see. I need to understand the cause of the symptoms in order to know how to treat the girl. Will this ruse keep him talking long enough to find out what I need?

I hear movement toward the door. After talking to the chemist, I would wean this make-believe baby off the opium and alcohol slowly with a diluted dosage of what I provide the women of Whitechapel who Francine brings into New Hope. Their alcohol withdrawal would be horrendous otherwise. With the baby, I would also have an on-call wet nurse to build up the baby's strength with mother's milk, not the goat's milk they received. I rap again.

A woman's voice, groggy with sleep, says through the door, "It's late, go away, come back tomorrow."

"I am Doctor Ryan Broadhead. I must consult with Doctor Meherhomji on an urgent matter. This can't wait." I can be a pompous West Ender when I need to be.

"One moment."

Two locks are opened, and an unshaven face peers out the door at about chest level. "How did you know how to find me?"

"I learned your name and description from the night nurse at Mrs. Burrough's house. She no longer works there, I understand. It was only a matter of time before one of your Indian patients from the neighborhood pointed me here. Do you want to know why I am knocking at your door after midnight?"

He doesn't open the door wider. I just made the mistake of telling him it was Alice who described him. The same Alice who had two baby girls die under her supervision.

I wait.

He stares. Sleep is leaving his brain. He is deciding if his curiosity outweighs his caution. The door opens further; I see in the dim light from somewhere behind the door, he is in his nightclothes. "What brings you here at this hour?"

"A baby girl adopted by my best friend's daughter and husband. I've known Phillip since my boarding school days; he summoned me to find out why the baby is in such agony."

"What's that have to do with me?" The door closes to where I can only see his face. I know the next question might cause it to close completely.

"The girl was sleepy when they brought her to their estate in Kent, and she has been crying non-stop ever since."

"Return her to Mrs. Burrough. I will be sure they will have another one with no issues in a week to ten days."

His answer tells me what I already know. He will give Burrough a remedy to wean a new baby off of laudanum and maybe put her on a breast. I am not sure I like this baby return policy. I hope my rising anger is not flushing my neck and cheeks.

"No, my good man, that won't work. The baby has Phillip's daughter's coloring. They don't want anyone to know the baby is not theirs. They've been sequestered in Kent for the past eight months. Phillip wants society to accept this baby as his grand-daughter when they return to London. He is begging me to find out what's wrong."

"That's the best I can do, Doctor Broadhead. Now, if you don't mind, I am going back to bed." He closes the door and before he can secure the first lock, my exploding anger directs my foot to slam the door back into him, sending him to the carpet. This is so unlike me, but not unlike someone who inhab-ited my body from the time I was five years old until last month. Looking down at his prone form on the parlor floor, it takes all my willpower not to stomp him senseless. The noise brings his wife into the room. I point a finger at her to not take another step

"Think again, Doctor Meherhomji. Two baby girls died in that house, and another is in terrible agony. If this one dies, I will have my friend the police superintendent rain holy hell upon you and Burrough. You will help me, or you will never practice medicine in this city again, as God is my witness."

"I can't," he sputters.

"You will." I reach for the poker from the fireplace. "I just made you an offer. I am taking it back. You have one bad leg. Do you want another?" I raise it above my head. What Hyde did to Carew is what I will do to this man's good leg if he doesn't give me the answer I already know. When did I become angry and violent?

"She keeps the baby girls sedated with laudanum. It takes a week to ten days to wean them off of the dose. It's possible this one was more..."

"More what?" I raise the poker higher.

"Please, no," he says as he tries to shield his face with his forearm.

"More what?" I snarl. My brain is rejecting this assault, but my body knows what it is like to beat someone with cane.

"More addicted," he confesses.

"And the two who died?"

"Ask Mrs. Burrough. I've nothing to do with their deaths."

I believe him, but I am not done with him yet. "Who administers the drug to the baby girls?"

"Mrs. Burrough does. She sends the dayshift nurse home at six and goes onto the girl's floor before the night shift nurse arrives at seven. Her daughter changes the girls' bedclothes while Burrough gives them their sleep medicine. She's an odd one, that girl, always singing nursery rhymes." He is crying now. I am tall, strong and angry. I lower the poker. I am getting answers.

"What other foundling houses do you visit?"

The question throws him.

"None, I swear."

Quieter now, I ask, "Does she give the boys any of the laudanum?"

"Not that I am aware of. They are how she makes her money."

I place the poker back in its holder next to the fireplace. I reach my hand down to him and help him to his feet. He is unsteady, and I guide him to his chair—unless his wife smokes a pipe on the reading stand next to it. I take her chair and lean in. "Tell me how she makes her money."

He does, and I become dizzy with the possibilities of what happened to Rosie's baby boy.

29

The largest city in the world is really nothing more than a collection of neighborhoods. Whitechapel is a microcosm of this greater mosaic. I should know. I've walked these streets from one end to the other. Anywhere there is gin to be sold and women offering their bodies for money, I have trodden. As people arrive here from their home countries, they flock together around their churches and shops selling foods and goods they know. Chinatown is tucked in near to the river, a Jewish ghetto with kosher food here, a Polish enclave with many pork sausages hanging in the shop windows there, and so it is with every nationality coming for a better life to this teeming metropolis.

Sadly in our search, Scots have a head start on the other groups. Intermarriage and business formation have blurred geographic and economic boundaries. Mary McCreary and I are looking for a red-headed needle in a haystack of redheads between the Scots and the Irish populating this slice of London. Internally, the Scottish rivalry between the Highlanders and the flatlanders borders on outright animosity with their incessant need for bragging rights, but they all will close ranks when an outsider is trying to find one of their own. Celeste Pirie will not be easy to find today, and it may take spreading some money around to refresh memories or loosen tongues.

I am exhausted from my early morning with Sally in Whitechapel. We returned with Molly. We came across her, bloody and defiled, in a gutter where no street lights shone. A roving gang took their fists and boots to her—to make her forget their faces and appendages. The women of the Whitechapel nights know all too well that raping a prostitute is not a rhetorical question, but convincing the police to take a report and begin an investigation would be fruitless.

We had to bribe a cabbie with a double fare to speed us to the Jekyll mansion. Alice worked with Henry to bandage Molly and apply balms. A split lip and broken ribs will heal, but the memories of what they did to her will haunt her for the rest of her life.

Louise was not happy to see me leave, what with Molly recovering from her injuries and going into alcohol withdrawal. Alice is still reeling from the deaths of the two baby girls. Lucy was colicky too. Henry did not have a moment to tell me about finding the Indian doctor. His sad puppy face could rival Lucky's when I told them I was closing my connecting door from my side. He promised to tend to Molly with Alice's help when she awakes. When I first met Doctor Jekyll, I wanted only his money to make the New Hope Mission a reality. I never dreamed how that meeting would change our lives.

All this turmoil in one night, and here I am running off to find a missing child. Yes, the baby is Rosie's. The baby is Mr. Murphy's niece, and, as I told Seamus last evening, I am no longer doing this work out of obligation to either of them. Mary McCreary and I made a promise to Rosie to find Baby James, and we live up to our promises. I look at what Mary has been through and what I have suffered. We take stock of our lives presently. I cannot think of two more qualified women to scour Whitechapel for the Pirie girl.

Last evening, Seamus and I were alone in the house where I was never welcome after Rosie moved in, and definitely not after my blackout. Dare I call it our first actual heart to heart after we went our separate ways by his choosing? Since the night he encountered me among the streetwalkers, our conversations have been laced with unspoken emotional baggage and seasoned with ember-hot anger. We sat at a table where we had shared our dreams and aspirations and instead talked, maybe for the first time, about some harsh realities. We could never talk like that in front of Rosie, and as my pregnancy became more difficult, my husband became more distant, and I retreated into the bottle. I am different now, and Seamus doesn't know what to make of me. Last night was an opportunity for him to see me as I am. Finding Baby James will determine what happens next between us.

Mary and I start to look for Celeste a few blocks away from the ominous Burrough house, which we avoided. Neither of us want to start our morning with a sense of dread weighing us down.

Almost immediately, we realize our Irish brogues, no matter how soft, heighten suspicion regardless of how benign our reasons are for finding Celeste. Going to Constable Collier will do us no good. What are we to do?

"I have an idea," Mary say.

Two hours later, we start at the other end of our search area accompanied by Fiona McTavish. She carries a carpet bag and her travelling clothes are smudged with dust. Both Mary McCreary and I are similarly dressed and are weighed down by leather-strapped suitcases in both hands.

We open the gates of the nearest church and find a sexton sweeping the front steps. "Sorry, could ye tell us hoo tae get doon tae the Pirie home," Fiona asks.

"Don't recognize the name, meself," he says. "But a parishioner, Jamie Frasure, might." Luckily, the Frasure house he points to is across the road and at the corner. Fiona leads us while we drag our luggage there.

Fiona knocks on the door, and we hear shuffling inside. A stooped man of at least eighty greets us with milky eyes and wild hair. "Ou might ye be?"

"Fiona Macleod and me sisters Mary and Francine. We've come doon from Dunvegan to be with me sister's daughter, Celeste Pirie, in her time of need."

"Ou don't have her address?" He squints away the sun behind us.

Fiona looks at me and shakes her head. "In her purse, stolen from the train."

Mary turns to give me a sour look, and I am properly chastised for losing it.

He shakes his head. "Pirie, Pirie, Can't say I know them. Wait here. I know who might."

We set our bags down. I feel like I really did take the overnight train from Glasgow and walked from the station to here. Both of my accomplices are wearing hats, but when you have thick red hair and are pretending to be a Highlander, you don't cover it up.

"Tell Dougie Campbell, ah sent ye."

"What's he do?" Fiona asks.

"A wee bit of everything, ah don ask." The elderly man nodded.

We nodded. Mary nudges Fiona. "Aye, Celeste's man is Archie."

"Archie what?"

"Just Archie is all we know."

"Ah know some Archies but they are all born and raised here, married too."

We shrug. He shrugs.

The address several blocks away is a pool room. Men slouch on chairs with sticks in their hands. A few are playing, but it is more of a social gathering place for loungers and reprobates.

Fiona and Mary march in. "Dougie Campbell," Mary says. She practiced his name with Fiona a few times while we trudged there.

"Ouse askin'?" a bowler-hatted, waxed mustached smoothy sets down his cue on the nearest table.

"Fiona Macleod from Dunvegan." She holds the slip of paper high above her head. "Jamie Frasure said Dougie would help us." Mary nudges a lounger to make room on the bench, and she drops onto it and releases her suitcases to the floor with a thump. I set mine down too, but remain standing.

"Frasure, you say?"

"Aye," she says as she hands it to him.

He studies it and, without saying a word, walks to the rear of the hall and disappears behind into a room dimly lit by book-keeper lamps. It's the counting room, and I immediately understand what Frasure meant by a 'wee bit of everything.'

A barrel-chested man with strawberry colored hair and a trim beard approaches us. Tall and thick, he would block out the sun if we were on the street. "What can I do for you?"

Fiona says, "Please, Dougie, we've come down on the Glasgow train to be with my sister's daughter, Celeste Pirie." She points to me. "She had the address in her purse until it was taken on the train. We went to the first church we saw, and they pointed us to Jamie Frasure, who pointed to you."

Looking at me, he asks, "How much money was in it?"

I wasn't prepared to speak. "Ah, ah, ah."

"She stutters awfully," Fiona says. "Not much, a pound, ten shillings and a few pence,"

He snaps his fingers, and one of his men peels off a five-pound note. "Here, don't lose this."

I look sheepishly at my cohorts. They nod. I take the note and bow my head and give a little curtsey.

"Can I get you tea and something to eat?" he asks.

"Tea would be nice. We breakfasted on the train," Fiona replies.

He snaps his fingers again and directs us to sit at a card table. The seats were warmed by the men playing cards, who abruptly end their game in mid-hand and fade into the woodwork.

"I'll send a runner to have her come here," he says.

The three women facing him smile gratefully.

"I'll be back to my business now, eh?" He disappears to the backroom and leaves us to wait for the tea and Celeste Pirie.

Before our tea gets cool enough to drink, the backroom door opens. Mary and Fiona have the backs turned to the door, and I see a young red-headed woman peering through the cigarette smoke at them. The confused look tells me our little game will soon end.

"Fiona, leave your bag and walk home now. I think they will be onto us shortly," I say as I nod toward the door. She turns and immediately ciphers out the situation. She gets up and does as I say.

Campbell, the woman and two of his men approach Mary and me.

"Celeste Pirie?" I ask without a hint of a stutter.

"Ouse asking?" She stares at us with no recognition.

I take the money out of my pocket, place it on the table and say to Dougie Campbell, "I would have placed this in the nearest poor box and said it was from you when I lit a candle for you. You are kind and generous. Thank you."

An amused smile creases the hard man's face. "And you?"

"Francine Murphy, and this is my friend Mary McCreary. We are searching for James O'Sullivan, a baby taken from the Burrough house last week. Celeste, please tell us what you know about that. I am sure Mr. Campbell would be interested in hearing what you have to say."

Who needs a constable present when a man who does a 'little of everything' and who counts money in the back room of a pool hall is staring at you.

"What is it to you?" she spits her question at me.

"Before Rosie married O'Sullivan, she was a Murphy. She's my husband's sister. She asked me to find out who stole her baby boy."

"I don't know what you are talking about," she says, suddenly afraid of where this is going.

I look at Dougie Campbell. "You might have heard of me. I walk the streets of Whitechapel almost every night rescuing ladies who have given up on themselves and have given in to the drink."

One tough tugs on his sleeve and whispers into his ear. He listens intently and says to me, "Aye, the do-gooder. Aye, I know of ye."

"I thought little happens in Whitechapel you were not aware of, so this stolen baby would interest you, no? Celeste was the night nurse on the girl's floor. Her boyfriend Archie would come and fetch her Sunday mornings for church, or so I heard. He knew his way around the building when everybody was asleep—how to get in and out with no one noticing," I am stretching on that last fact. "Mrs. Burrough fired her shortly after the baby went missing."

Campbell turned to Pirie and growled, "Is that true?"

"I didn't steal no baby," Celeste cries.

"And Archie, was he trying to help a young childless couple out for a few quid?" I ask.

Four pairs of angry eyes and a pair of sad eyes are staring at the young redhead. All activity in the pool room comes to a halt. Mary McCreary says softly, "How awful for you, dearie."

"You'll have to ask him; we are not together anymore."

Mary reaches over to Celeste and takes her hands. "Tell us what you know while we send someone for him."

Campbell glares at the lassie, and she spits out an address and workplace in one heaving breath. The two men standing on either side of her depart.

Mary guides Celeste to a chair at the card table. Campbell takes a seat facing the door, and I sit across from him. I catch his eye as Mary soothes Celeste. An ace of hearts sits face up on the sloppy deck of cards. "Remind me never to play poker with ye." His eyes are smiling at me.

30

Louise helps Molly realize her future would be brighter if she stayed at the New Hope Mission until she is better. Alice re-wraps the bandages around Molly's ribs. The nasty black bruises with the greenish tint stretching from hip to armpit will fade, eventually. I tell her not to laugh. The swelling on her lower lip has not gone down, and she smiles slightly. I give her a remedy that helps with alcohol withdrawal, and I tell her what to expect. While Alice applies new bandages to Molly's elbows and knees, she recounts the night she came to stay with us and how she saved Lucy's life. If anything, the new lady in our house is learning it is a safe place to heal. I have quietly observed how Francine and Louise talk with the new ladies when they first come to stay with us. There is no sermonizing. No recriminations. No talk of eternal damnation and hellfire. No talk of debts owed. No talk of families destroyed by their drinking and prostitution. Everything is private in this house. What is said here, stays here. Francine and Louise quote Mary McCreary the way preachers pound on the pulpit with chapters and verses from the Bible. 'You are not the person you were (yesterday), (last week), (last month).' 'You are winning the battle with the devil and are getting stronger every day.' 'Nothing can stop you from starting over.' 'Your future starts today.' 'No looking back.' 'Yesterday is gone.' 'You can't change the past; move on.' 'You are not that person anymore.' Ladies with no self-worth weaning off of alcohol require lots of handholding. The other women, who are a little further down the path, encourage the new ladies to follow along. Slowly, a new woman emerges from the past shell of themselves. Only then will Francine ask them to accompany her where the Siren's call. The ladies on the street are astonished to see one of their own all cleaned up, sober and showing what the first steps out of hell look like.

After she is cleaned up, Molly is invited to breakfast. Lucky is her companion while we make our way to the kitchen. How does he know she needs a friend?

Will I ever tire of the wondrous smells greeting my nostrils every morning? I must enjoy these moments while I can. It won't be long before the space in Whitechapel is ready and it will be just Francine, Lucky, Lucy, Poole and me. I must hire one lady to be our cook. What if Francine returns to her husband? Will she take the dog? What if we find Lucy's family and they want her?

What if it is only Poole and me? What was acceptable for a proper West End bachelor upon my return from the islands leaves me sorely bereft. The possibility of losing Francine, my four-legged companion, and the swirl of activity in this house drops me into a funk. What am I to make of the warm kiss goodnight before the door closed on me in the early morning hours? Was it a parting kiss of a promising future or of a fleeting moment of passing love?

Before Louise and I visit the future home of The New Hope Mission, I have an appointment with Utterson at the General Register Office. What Meherhomji told me about the babies he pronounced dead at the Burrough house sent chills to my bones. Utterson wanted more proof before he called in Scotland Yard, and he told me it would be found at the GRO. For over fifty years, all births, marriages and deaths in England and Wales have been recorded there. He told me he would put his order in when the building opens and would threaten not to leave until they gave him what he wanted. My lawyer could be very persuasive. Ferocious in the courtroom, but convivial with magistrates and parliamentarians at social events and private dinners, he knew how to curry favor. Should he receive anything else except an enthusiastic response there, he would not hesitate to call in a marker.

The message I received late morning was to proceed with all due haste. After 1874, a physician was required to list a cause of death on the certificate. What has Utterson found?

31

"Start from the beginning." Mary is patting Celeste's hand. I place a still cooling cup of tea in front of the shaken girl. The card table's felt is worn where elbows press against the edges. No place for the former night nurse to hide her cards.

"I took the job cuz it was simple, really. I watched them girls sleep all night. The ninny would come in towards morning and help me change the outfits, all twenty of them, before the day nurse came in."

"The ninny?" I asked.

"Mrs. Burrough's daughter, what's her name?" Celeste looked to the peeling ceiling in a show of memory loss. "Always with the rhymes, never shuts up, that one. I still kin hear scampering up and down the stairs all night. Gave me the chills. She'd take the soiled clothes and bedsheets to the laundry after we was dun." Celeste took a sip of tea. "Needs sugar."

No one at the table was offering her any sweetness. "What else?" Mary asked quietly but firmly.

"They are easy, them girls. Nothin' to do. None of them fussed one bit. Like changin' a ragdoll. None of them moved a muscle."

179

"Why's that?" Mary asked.

"Mrs. Burrough fed them herself. Put somethin' in their bottle, suppose."

"Any idea what?" I ask.

"Dunno, but it knocked them out all night."

"Whisky?" Campbell asked.

"No, I would have smelled that when one of them threw up," she replied. "Only happened a couple of times with the older ones before…." She took a sip of tea. "Before they died. Guess they were sick. When I saw one of them wasn't movin', I would send the nin—Felicity, that's her name, I would send Felicity to fetch her mother."

"And then what?"

"She would come in and agree with me, and she would call the doctor in the morning."

"How many?" Campbell asked. He was tumbling onto what was going on at that house of horrors.

"Five, six, at the least. The newest babies came into the room above her office, and them's there the longest were put in the room by the back stairs."

"What about the boys?" I asked. I knew the way the boys' beds were arranged were the opposite of what Celeste just told us.

She shrugged. "There was less of 'em, but their night nurse was always busy. When I heard one of 'em cryin', I'd come down to help. Seems like Mrs. Burrough put the new boys by the back stairs. Wonder why that was?"

I had an idea, but I wanted her to explain it herself.

"When a boy's ma didn't come back to claim 'im, he was adopted out just like the contract said, 'twas what Archie tumbled onto. He explained it to me."

"Rosie's baby was paid up for a year. If she doesn't come back from America to claim him, Mrs. Burrough could put him up for adoption." I explain this to Doug Campbell.

"How many of the women don't come back for their wee ones?" he asks.

"I dunno," Celeste says. She is looking calmer now, even though we are talking about Baby James.

Mary withdraws her hand from Celeste's free hand on the table. "Answer him truthfully, dearie."

Celeste places both hands in her lap and looks down. "None of them come back for their babies, Mr. Campbell. None of them. She would adopt the boys out when their mother didn't come back. They had parents waiting for 'em. Thems were happy days when the boys left in the arms of their new parents. Felicity was excited when she got to dress the boys up in their new baby clothes. She'd make up a rhyme just for them and sing it all night long. Drove me batty."

"And what about the girls?" Doug asks.

"Dunno any girls getting adopted unless Mrs. Burrough could convince a couple to take one too."

Mary says, "He's asking what happened when the girls' contracts ran out and there was no one waiting to adopt them."

Celeste scrunches her forehead in thought. More like she couldn't puzzle out the questions. "Nothing; those girls died months before they could be adopted. May I have more tea?"

The three wiser adults at the table understood full well the implications of what Celeste said without her giving it any deeper thought. I could see why Mrs. Burrough hired her.

Doug looked at me. I nodded. He turned to Mary. She swallows and nods. He snaps his fingers. "More tea for the lass...and sugar."

"Like I said, it was a simple job. Not much to do at night," she says.

"So why were youse fired?" Doug asks.

"A big misunderstanding, Mister Campbell. Mrs. Burrough thought I had somethin' to do with the missing baby. I swear on all that is holy, I had nothing to do with it."

Before Doug or I can question her further, Mary says. "I believe you, deary. When you tell us you had nothing to do with it, you didn't, but here's the rub. Tell us how your man could have something to do with it."

The tea arrives; the water must have been boiling atop a blast furnace. Celeste cools it off with some milk and a generous heaping or two of sugar, and she stirs it sensibly before testing it. She stares at the cup and saucer. I hope she tells us before it cools off.

The door to the back room opens, and the two men Doug sent for Archie are standing there. "'Scuse me, ladies," he says.

We watch the animated conversation taking place. Celeste is closest to the door and could outrun Mary and me, but she is leaning in to catch what is being said.

He returns, and his men flank him. "Seems Archie is no longer aboot the 'Chapel. The leather shop hasn't seen him since payday."

Mary grabs Celeste's hand fiercely. "Save the tears for later; tell us now what we want to know."

The words spill out like a river overflowing its banks. "I don't know. He could have taken the baby, I don't know. On Sunday mornings, it was quiet in the house. He would come and fetch me for church. I was his girl, and he wanted to show the world, but then he would come earlier, sometime while it was dark. I let him in through the root cellar door. We would visit there. Nobody knew we were there, not even the ninny. He would go back outside when it got light out, and I would go check on the girls before he would come back at quittin' time."

"But it was cold and damp there, and you took a chance at havin' him come up the back steps to the third floor where it was warm and you had a nice couch to sit on," I say.

"More than a few times, right dearie?" Mary asks.

"But Felicity caught you, and you told her she could never tell her mother. It was your secret with her," I say.

"That was until Baby James went missing, and now your Archie is missing."

"Yes! Yes! All of that is true." Celeste wails. "After she fired me, I told Archie the baby was missing and asked him if he had taken it, and he said no, and I believed him. Then he stopped calling on me, and we didn't see him in church. I don't know what to think." Her tears fall into her teacup. No comfort came from the seated women or standing men.

"Where is Archie Rathbone?" Doug asks.

"I dunno," Celeste says. "Can you find him, Mr. Campbell? Can you find him for me?"

"Did he ever talk about taking a baby?" Mary asks.

Celeste shook her head. "No, never."

"It looks like Archie kidnapped Rosie O'Sullivan's baby. He could swing for that," Doug says. "Now if ye could get the baby back unharmed, Mrs. Murphy wouldn't press charges against him."

"Maybe ye can get Archie back too," Mary says.

"But I dunno where he is. I swear." Celeste pleads her innocence. "Find him, please."

"If your man has fled the 'Chapel, I doon have many favors I kin ask across the river."

"He's lived here all his life; I don't know where he would go," she says. "He'd be lost."

"Not with some money in his pocket," Doug says abruptly. "Mrs. Murphy, it was nice meeting you and your friend Mary, but I have other pressing business."

"Should you, by chance, learn of Archie's whereabouts, you can leave a message for me at McCreary's," I say.

"I know the store," he says.

"Let's walk you home, dearie. You've had a terrible day," Mary says.

The meeting is over. Archie is missing. Baby James is missing, and before the money runs out, innocent baby girls die at the Burrough house like turning a page on the wall calendar.

We step outside into sleet and rain. Not a cab to be found.

32

The directions given to me by the information desk send me through a labyrinth of hallways, and I must ask again and again until I see Utterson seated in a meeting room at a long table across from the General Register Office. Is it the glass or does he look pale? I open the door and confirm my friend and counselor looks ill. He limply points to a stack of papers and says, "I want you to see for yourself what goes on in the Burrough house."

He rubs his face with a handkerchief and sits back with a look like his dog just ran out in the street and was run over. I've met him for business and on social occasions over half my life and never saw him this way. The wind is completely out of his sails. "They go back to '75—almost thirteen full years. Burrough's husband died in '72."

The first thing I notice on the death certificates is that of the Burrough house address. Whoever did the sorting had their hands full. First, they needed to look at just the city of London, then the section of Whitechapel, then this specific address. The stack is easily a foot tall of single page death certificates. Thirteen years of deaths at this one location.

"Just the Burrough address, I see."

He nods.

"There must be hundreds," I say

"One hundred and twenty-three," he says.

"My God!" I set the top pages back on the stack. I feel like I am touching festering boils from the Black Plague. I am not sure I want to proceed.

Utterson doesn't look at me. Instead, he gets up and stretches the weariness from his bones. "They are separated by year and by sex. Go on, see for yourself."

I silently count eight died in 1875, one boy and seven girls. For each year thereafter, the total number increase but the percentage of boys to girls varies insignificantly. I am appalled but not surprised. Breastfeeding one group and watering down goat's milk for the others accounts for some of that difference. Illnesses are listed as the cause of death. The girls would have no immunity against infection and disease. I will have to talk to Alice and learn from Francine how they cared for the girls differently than the boys. Then there is the matter of the girls being drugged into constant sleep. Legs and arms don't move. Lungs don't develop. Malnutrition. It's a wonder any of them lived past six months. I create separate stacks for each year and separate the boys from the girls. In recent years, I seen only one signature for the attending physician. It is the man I knocked to the floor of his own flat and threatened with a fire poker. It is the physician who purchases enough laudanum to sedate horses. I see a disturbing pattern. Age at time of death skews towards eleven months. After what their doctor told me, I am surprised any of them made it that far. What was missing were pronouncements of malnutrition or infectious diseases. Not a single finding of neglect or infanticide. That goes without saying. If the doctor was doing his job honestly, he would be implicating himself with those pronouncements when the authorities came to arrest Mrs. Burrough.

At eleven months, almost every manner of death is listed as natural causes, and every cause of death is listed as heart failure.

I step away from the stacks. I walk over to Utterson, who refuses to return my gaze. The horror is too much for him. As a trained physician, I am barely controlling my despair and anger. "When the money runs out, the girls die to make room for more paying customers."

He coughs in agreement.

"The boys are the milch cows. She gets money at both ends."

He states in agreement, "Lose a boy and lose money. Lose a girl and make more money."

"The woman who gave birth to a baby girl was headed there. Either way, Burrough would have made money," I say, "except she was robbed of her purse. She had no money for Mrs. Burrough to care for her baby."

"Maybe she was turned away by Mrs. Burrough." Utterson is returning to form now that he has me to share the horror laying in neat stacks on the table.

"The night nurses would know if she came knocking when she was about to deliver." I imagine the terror of the young woman with no money, no place to go, no place to rest when she went into labor.

I turn to look at the table and see the number of sheets bearing Dr. Meherhomji's signature on death certificates of girls dying in their eleventh month of natural causes from heart failure separated from the rest of the stacks. I must count them, and my hands tremble. "Did you?"

Utterson says, "Yes, but I need you to verify my count is correct."

My breathing comes in quick gasps, and my eyes mist over. "Twenty-nine."

"Same."

———

After Mary McCreary and I walk Celeste home, we find Archie's address and, rather than repeat the process of Dougie Campbell's men, we visit with their neighbors on either side and decide to take advantage of their dislike for young Archie. A few shillings change hands and promises are made to alert us if the smart-arse (their words, not mine) shows his face. Same process over by the leather shop.

The rain slackens, and we change back into our regular clothes. Gabby and Paddy will run the store while Mary and I take a cab over to the future home of New Hope Mission. We've gone over the possibilities. What if Celeste is telling the truth? What if she had no clue what Archie was up to? We must find out who Archie sold the baby to and get Seamus to identify the infant, then our work is over. Hanging over us like dark clouds spitting icy rain is the startling revelation Burrough is killing off the girls. The Ripper killed as many women as Celeste guessed baby girls died under that roof during her time there. How many more have died? And I am not talking at the hands of Saucy Jack? The world over waits with hushed breath for more grisly deaths to be reported by the man I know will never kill again, yet Mrs. Burrough goes about her business of fostering babies until the contracts expire. Some get adopted, and others don't see their first birthday. All done behind closed doors with no one the wiser.

We pull up just as Henry and Louise are alighting from their carriage. "How's Molly?" I ask.

Louise says, "Better after sleeping in a proper bed. The good doctor and Alice changed her dressings, and he gave her a remedy for her withdrawals. Sally, Agatha, and Jane did not go to market today cuz of the rain, so they are there for both Molly and Alice."

"How's Lucy?" I ask Louise.

Instead, Henry answers me, "The wet nurse arrived just as I was leaving. Lucy took to the breast immediately, and when I returned she was sleeping peacefully. It was hard leaving her to come here."

Never heard him say that before. I know Henry has a soft spot in his heart for our dog and the baby, but I am surprised by his focus on Lucy today.

"We are to meet this afternoon at Utterson's office to discuss our findings after we finish with the contractor. There are some changes I want to propose," he says.

The contractor is completing our final changes, and Henry appears preoccupied. He walks over to the southern wall and paces off most of it. He turns to the contractor and says. "Window, I want window all along here." Every four paces, he points. "Here." The contractor chalks out heights and widths. "I want water basins here, here and here." The measuring stick goes this way and that. "Floor to ceiling closets, cedar here and here. Pine here and here." The contractor cannot keep up with him. Henry is a man on a mission.

Mary, Louise and I stare at him as he redesigns half of the first floor square footage. The meeting space between the baking kitchen and these new oversized rooms is now half of what it was. My head is spinning with the changes. Louise had the benefit of riding to this building with him and is not questioning any of it. What had been my thoughts for the nursery have just been expanded fourfold.

I hear him saying to the harried contractor. "We need suitable space for fifty infants. Do you understand me?"

33

The cab roof covers us from the sleet and rain that picked up as darkness set in. Henry sits next to me and reaches for my hand under the blanket covering our legs. I sit across from Mary, and Louise is facing Henry. The news Mary and I have about Baby James is not good. Worse, Celeste told us that five or six baby girls had died on her overnights. She worked for Mrs. Burrough for much of the year.

Is Henry shaking from the cold or from his findings at the General Register Office? He keeps repeating the number twenty-nine and shakes his head. Louise apparently knows what that number signifies, and her face shows as much sorrow as his. She didn't object once when Henry paced out measurements on the first floor of New Hope Mission and had the contractor carve out as much space for the nursery as for the kitchen and parlors together. We will be arriving at Utterson's office in another fifteen minutes. This weather has dampened business along the route our cabbie takes. Folks are hidden under their umbrellas as they dart from overhang to overhang.

We should be excited as construction is starting round the clock. Instead, dread fills my thoughts. Scanning the faces of those around me, I can see the goings-on at the Burrough house are on their minds too. We ride in silence.

Utterson walks us up three flights of stairs to the attic. Below the front and back slopes of the roof sits a long antique table underneath the trusses Henry has to duck under. How it got up here in one piece would be a test of strength and balance for the men bringing it up those winding stairs.

"Tell us about your meeting with Celeste Pirie," Utterson says, with pencil hovering notepad.

I nod to Mary to proceed.

"She's not the brightest lassie, but that helps me believe she is being mostly honest. A local racketeer named Doug Campbell helped us find her and put the fear of the devil in her. Here is the address of the pool hall where he runs his businesses. He was very helpful, actually."

By now, anything Mary McCreary and I do does not surprise the men, Henry particularly. Meeting with a racketeer or a Scotland Yard inspector is all in a day's work for me.

Mary continues. "Regarding her gentleman caller, Archie Rathbone, absconding with Rosie's baby, he had access to the boy when he went up and down the backstairs to be with Celeste on those lonely overnights."

"I believed Campbell's footmen when they told us Archie left with his last paycheck," I say. "Celeste doesn't know where he is, isn't sure Archie took the baby and asked Campbell to find him for her."

"How much money would a desperate couple pay for a healthy baby boy?" Utterson asks.

"Mr. and Mrs. Blackwell must visit the Burrough house and find out the going rate," Henry says.

"I am not sure I want to return there," I respond to my make-believe husband. "I am getting nightmares about something bad happening to Lucy. I keep seeing Mrs. Burrough and her daughter in my dreams."

"I would purposely walk on different streets to avoid that house," Mary says.

"Sell the baby and flee the country with the proceeds. Sounds like Archie took advantage of the situation his sweetheart was in," Louise says.

"Is it enough money to risk getting marched up the gallows?" Utterson asks.

"He probably thought Mrs. Burrough wouldn't report the disappearance," I say.

"From what we know about the goings on at the Burrough house on the girl's floor, I understand why Mrs. Burrough didn't report the boy's disappearance," Henry says.

I say, "Rosie waited a day before doing so, hoping her baby would magically return."

"Burrough fired Celeste after the boy went missing," Mary says.

"And Archie is nowhere to be found," Utterson says.

"And he vanished with his final pay in his pocket," I say.

"Even if he didn't do that, I would say Mrs. Burrough would blame Celeste," Henry says.

"Burrough's daughter Felicity probably told her mother about Archie coming and going," Mary says. "This could be her way of blaming Archie and Celeste when Rosie unexpectedly returned with the rest of the money."

"From what we know about the girl, she probably listened to what Archie and Celeste did to pass the time on these chilly nights. She runs about the house barefoot and knows every step in the back stairways," I say. "She knows all the hiding places, I would wager."

"What is it about her?" Louise asked.

"The girl is touched in the head—runs about the house repeating rhymes," Mary says.

The women and the lawyer look at Henry for a medical opinion.

"From what I remember, there can be many causes, but didn't someone tell us, Mrs. Burrough is not a widow; her husband left her after he witnessed Felicity's behaviour," he says.

"The laundress or one of the wet nurses," I say. "We should be writing this all down."

"I am, for reasons we will explain shortly," Utterson says.

There is more sleet than rain now as the temperature drops. Only the heat rising from the downstairs fireplaces keeps us from shivering. It pounds the roof above us with the percussion of a regimental drum corps. The sleet is telling us we need more hard facts. We can't let the rain dilute our assumptions.

"Mrs. Burrough never expected Rosie to return to pay what she still owed. She could have sold the baby to a couple like Mrs. Blackwell and me for a premium. Then when she found out the baby was missing, her exact words, she blamed Celeste and her beau," Henry says. "I would have written out a check to get a baby boy immediately. I would have paid an extra fee. What's stopping Mrs. Burrough from making a quick sale? When Rosie turned up, she was forced to blame Celeste."

"Maybe Archie did his sums and felt he was being set up," Utterson says. "He never took the baby but was afraid he would be framed for the kidnapping."

"How much is a beautiful, healthy Irish boy worth?" Mary asks.

Henry looks at me. "We have to return to that house to answer your question. I made the demand I skip the queue."

There is something about his urgency I don't understand. Before I can reply, Mary continues. "I am asking what price Archie could fetch on his own from a couple buying a boy."

"Whitechapel folks have no money and more babies being born to mothers without husbands. He wouldn't find a buyer around here," I say.

"So he would have to have buyers with a desperate need and lots of idle cash," Louise says.

"Someone like the Blackwells," Henry say.

"Maybe a customer from the leather shop," Mary says.

Utterson writes that down. "Yes, Henry, you and Francine must return to see Mrs. Burrough about setting the price, before…"

What else did Celeste tell you?" Henry interrupts. It is so unlike him to do that.

"The girls," Mary says. She reaches for her handkerchief and dabs her eyes.

I pat her free hand and look at the others. I take a deep breath and finish Mary's sentence.

"The girls die before the date their money runs out."

"How long did Celeste work overnights with the girls?" Utterson asks.

"Much of the year, no exact dates," Mary answers.

"How many girls did she say died?" Utterson asks.

Mary and I debate who will answer Henry's lawyer. "One more than the Ripper killed so far this year." To any Londoner and to most of the world where newspapers were printed, the number of known Ripper killings stood at five and counting.

Utterson says, "Would you be surprised if Celeste's memory was self-serving?"

Mary and I look at each other like we are bracing for the roof to collapse. "How many?"

"Twelve this year," Henry says. "Six of illness and unknown reasons and six in their eleventh month of natural death caused by heart disease."

"Twelve?" Mary asked.

"Six in their eleventh month — all the same manner and cause?" I am shocked. My visits to coroner's inquests of the Ripper's victims gave me an education into both the manner and cause of deaths.

"Since Doctor Meherhomji became the doctor for the Burrough house, twenty-nine girls have died a natural death in the eleventh month caused by heart disease."

Louise shakes her head upon hearing the number again. Mary and I look at each other in disbelief. Suddenly, I realize why Doctor Jekyll wants to make a space for fifty babies at New Hope Mission. He is planning to empty Mrs. Burrough's house and put her out of business.

"Francine, we have to go back there and find out how much time we have before the next girl is put to sleep permanently. Burrough is drugging the girls with laudanum and gives a double dose to the girls reaching the time when the money runs out to care for them," Henry says.

I nod. The nightmares I am having about the house of horrors just became real.

"We think Lucy's mother may have been turned away because she had been robbed and had no way of paying Mrs. Burrough," Utterson says.

"Thanks to Alice, Sally and you, Lucy is alive," Henry says to me.

No wonder Henry was so concerned about Lucy today. This could have happened to his baby, our baby girl, if the unknown woman came with the cash. Jack the Ripper killing twenty-nine women would paralyze London with fear. Twenty-nine persons lined up against a wall and shot would make headlines for such a heinous slaughter, but twenty-nine girls dying of natural causes in a house where they are abandoned doesn't raise any concerns, until now.

Utterson adds, "Mrs. Burrough may have lied to Constable Collier about Lucy's mother and to the first constable about Baby James going missing. You need more proof before calling in the police."

"Twenty-nine girls died before their first birthday. I will ask Collier to set up a meeting with Inspector Abberline," I say.

"We were thinking you would be the best person to talk to them," Utterson says.

Mary says, "I know why you go out every night to save the women from the streets, Francine. I know why we are keeping our promises to Seamus and Rosie to find her baby, but I need to ask if saving the boys and girls from that wretched house is too much."

"What would you rather we do?" asks Henry before I answer. In that moment, I realize it is no longer my mission, but it is his mission to save the babies. Does the shift in focus from Baby James to all the remaining babies at the foundling house take me further away from my promise to Rosie and my husband? Does Henry want to supplant my promise to them to bring him closer to me? Will caring for dozens of babies and still going out at night to convince women who sell their bodies for gin be our mission now?

Can I tell Seamus I know the name of the man who probably stole James O'Sullivan and sold him to a family who will care for him after Rosie abandoned him? If Rosie had had a baby girl instead, that baby would still be there. When Rosie and Mrs. Burrough reached the end of the contract for that baby, it would die of natural causes because of heart disease.

I look at those gathered around the table. How long was I in thought about my answer? "Yes, Mary, it is too much, and Henry is right when he asks what you would rather have us do."

"Leave it to Scotland Yard. Let them sort it out. I am concerned about you. I am worried about you," she says.

For Mary to admit her concerns about me tells me I have reached much further than my grasp. She has always encouraged me. This may be the first time she has cautioned me I am taking on too much responsibility. I realize she knows me better than anybody alive.

I say as much to myself as to her and those around the table. "I have Louise to help me with the ladies. I have Sally, Agatha and Jane to help me with the baking. I have Henry and Utterson to make sure we save those babies from Mrs. Burrough, and I have you to believe in me."

"I needed to hear you say that," Mary says.

Louise says, "Don't forget Alice can teach us to care for the babies." She is giving her support to the changes being proposed.

Henry looks into my eyes and says, "For as long as I live and breathe, I will stand with you."

We've been through much, Henry and I. Mary has always had my best interests at heart. She saved me from my despair and drinking. Louise believes in our mission. Utterson will guide us with all his wits and will.

The sleet pounds home our decision to include the Burrough house babies in our plans. "Don't ask me how I know this, but I have faith in us."

Utterson has the last word. "Mrs. Burrough left word she has a boy for you."

34

"I understand you have found a suitable heir to the Blackwell fortune," I say.

Francine sits next to me across from Mrs. Burrough. We are the rich couple who paid her a visit the previous week. We hold our saucers and teacups just so. The woman doesn't smile at my snide sense of humor.

"The child is ready for you to take home today. Your lawyer said you would be giving me cash. How do you propose caring for the infant until you return home?"

"The nurse is waiting in the carriage."

"When was the last time he was fed?" Francine asks.

"This afternoon before we dressed him for you," Burrough replies.

"May we go see him?" Francine asks.

"We have to complete the adoption contract and finish the transaction first, and then I will send for him," Burrough says.

"Not only do we want to see the child first, but my wife would like to visit the third floor."

As expected, her stern countenance becomes dour. She sits back in her high-backed winged chair. There is no answer forthcoming. A pall comes over the room. What should be a joyous occasion has become contentious to the point of stalemate. We set down our tea on the large desk and place our hands in our laps. Unseen by the seller of children is Francine's skirted knee bouncing up and down. The staring contest begins. My pleasant smile disappears. I try not to think about all the dead babies and my urge to reach across the desk and slap her hard.

Burroughs moves her right index finger to the file I believe contains all the paperwork to undertake the adoption and lifts one edge to close it. With a noticeable shrug, she says, "There are others waiting for this beautiful boy." She stands, takes the folder in both hands and turns to place it in the filing cabinet. This is where Constable Collier and Inspector Abberline will be looking immediately after all the babies are cleared out from upstairs. "Now if you excuse…"

Francine and I do not budge. Just then, Felicity bursts into the room—a bundle of wild energy barely constrained. "Baby boy all ready. Baby boy all ready. The baby boy is all ready for a new home." The singsong voice pronounces.

"Felicity, these people are not following rules. We know what happens when you don't follow the rules."

The look of terror on the young woman's face. "No, Mother, no!" She shields her face and head with her arms and cowers in the corner made by the fireplace and the center wall.

"Not you, Felicity, them." She points at Francine and me.

I am not sure if the command is directed at the terrorized child or all of us.

Felicity bolts from the room.

"Obviously, you are more concerned about your rules than the opportunity my darling wife wanted to pursue on the third floor." I stand to leave, and Francine gets up from her chair, haltingly. We are moving with no particular haste towards the front door.

"You would like to take a girl home too, Mrs. Blackwell?" Burrough sees the opportunity.

"Come along, my dear. There are other boys and girls waiting for a new home," I say.

"Edward," Francine pleads.

"Of course we can see your baby boy on our way up to the girls' floor." The change in demeanor is startling. Mrs. Burrough communicates with Francine to maintain the upper hand and salvage the situation. "This way." She points to the center stairway.

I take another step towards the front door and place my hat on my head.

Francine darts towards me and takes my right hand in both of hers. She looks up into my eyes. I know she is playing a part, but for that moment I survey her features and remind myself how lucky I am to have this woman in my world. I doubt any other woman will ever captivate me the way she does. I remove my hat, bow, and usher her to the stairs.

As with our last visit, the boy's cribs are arranged in the rooms from left to right with the newest additions by the back staircase. Felicity is hovering over the last crib. Mrs. Burrough clears her throat. Both the day nurse and the waif look up. One smiles, and the other darts into the stairwell and heads upstairs.

Before we reach the crib. Francine asks, "And what is your name, dear?"

The nurse is startled and looks to her employer for permission to speak. Burrough nods.

"Phyllis Parkins," she says.

"The Parkins of Mayfair?" Francine asks. Finding this woman later will be important to our plans.

She looks confused. "No, Mum, here." She points in the eastern direction.

"And how has our boy been for you? Any problems?"

Phyllis looks to Burrough for permission again to speak. "He's not been a problem. All good."

We make our way to the crib. No date, no star. An adorable child is staring back at us. I can't help but smile. I thought I was prepared for this moment, but I am not. My heart melts.

"He's beautiful," Francine says. She slips her arm around mine. It feels nice, it feels real, and we can enjoy this moment, for this child will not spend another day in this house of death. This foundling will have a loving home. Edward is the name we've chosen, and he and Lucy will grow up as brother and sister.

"May I hold him?" Francine asks.

This time the nurse doesn't need permission and lifts him from the spotless crib and hands him to Francine, who takes him in her arms the way she holds Lucy. He leans towards her breast with his mouth, and she quickly moves him to her shoulder. "Let's find you a sister."

The difference between the floors is like day and night. Active boys, alert and moving about. Quiet girls all appear to be sleeping, but subtly different from the way Lucy sleeps in her crib. These babies are sedated and not sleeping peacefully. Hunger in their thin frames is apparent. The closer to eleven months old, the more pronounced the decline in observable health. Burrough stops in front of a baby girl, but I keep moving to the last crib. We want to remove the girl whose date with a double dose of drugs is closest. Her bedclothes are the shabbiest. The day nurse for girls is seated in the room with the latest arrivals. She doesn't get up to acknowledge us. I know those girls are among the healthiest. They have been drugged for fewer days than this one we need to remove immediately.

Burrough moves in quickly. "I will need to contact her mother to allow for the adoption."

"How long does that usually take?" I don't take my eyes off of the baby girl. I want to memorize her features to prevent Burrough from making a switch.

"About ten days," Burrough replies. She knows the time to wean this child from laudanum. It strikes me how unusual and how ghastly her business is. I don't know how many girls go home with parents who came for a boy and leave with a girl as well. Why the other one and not this one? Mrs. Burrough is the angel of death, deciding who lives and who dies, but not today.

"I want to name her Alice," Francine says as she shifts Edward to her other shoulder and peers closer to the motionless infant. She then places him in my arms, and she makes a show out of how I should hold him, even though I have had plenty of practice with Lucy. I act like it is the first time, and I make a show of it.

She scoops the nearly lifeless form from the threadbare batting of the crib's interior and lifts the baby to her bare neck. The baby responds to the warmth of Francine's skin and her touch. This child is starving for more than nutrients. Burrough is occupied with the child's chart. Francine and I nod in silent agreement.

"Alice Blackwell is a good name. My father's oldest sister's name is Alice. She will be happy we thought of her." Like picking the Christmas goose at market, I declare, "We want this one." This man I portray is all about the family name. Status and wealth and keeping his new wife happy go hand in hand. "Now I am ready to hand you the cash," I say.

———

PHYLLIS PARKINS EXITS the foundling house through the front door minutes after we completed our paperwork for Edward. Funny how our delayed departures nearly coincides. Our wet nurse is breastfeeding Edward. We have one more seat in our covered carriage on this cold, moonless December night.

"Phyllis," Francine calls out from the carriage like she is calling her best friend.

The shawled young woman turns to the sidewalk, thinking the person is hailing her from street level.

"Here," Francine says. "Mr. Blackwell is offering you a lift home."

Our wet nurse is in on the ruse and busies herself with Edward as Phyllis climbs in. I say, "How fortunate to be heading in your direction. Give the driver your address."

She does, and I repeat it to the driver. Henry nods. "Did Mrs. Burrough tell you we selected a girl too? I am delirious with happiness." I say.

She sees the wet nurse and nods hello. "Yes, she did. Mrs. Burrough is happy to find a home for both children, and I am happy for you."

We have little time to talk as the address is only a few blocks away. "Why is it that your floor of boys is so cheery and alive, and the girl's floor is so drab and dreary?" I ask.

"It's much harder to find a home for the girls," she says.

Henry harrumphs, "Then why have more girls? From a business standpoint, it doesn't make sense?"

Phyllis shrugs and looks out the carriage, most probably to see how much longer she must ride with this wealthy couple and their nurse. Answering questions about her employer looks to make her nervous.

"Do you know anything about the girl we picked out? Mrs. Burrough was rather vague, wouldn't you say, dear?" I look at Henry.

"Like she doesn't spend any time on that floor," he says.

"But she does," Phyllis says, "every night after the day nurse leaves and before the night nurse comes on to give them their medicine."

"Medicine?" My voice raises an octave. "Are any of the girls sick?"

Phyllis says, "No, not really. It helps them sleep."

"You said 'not really' Miss Parkins. Did the girl we chose need to see a doctor?" Henry turns toward her with an alarmed posture.

"No, never on the girls' floor, only for the boys. Thank you for the ride, Mr. Blackwell, but I remembered I need to stop at the store before it closes. Let me out here, please." The driver halts his horses. She must cross over Henry and the nurse to alight from the carriage. She says, "Thank you again for the ride. You have nothing to worry about."

She is out of the carriage in a flash. She walks one way then crosses the street and turns the other way.

Henry says, "What she didn't want to tell us is the only time a doctor visits the girls' floor is to pronounce one of them dead."

The wet nurse doesn't know the whole story about the Burrough house, and her eyes widen. Baby Edward stops sucking and cries. He must have felt the poor woman's alarm.

I wait until the noise of hooves on cobblestones drowns out my words in Henry's ear. "There is more that woman can tell Scotland Yard."

He turns and whispers, "We need to contact them sooner than later, I can wean Baby Alice off of the drugs. We have what we came for."

"What about Baby James?" I ask.

"What could we have said or asked of Parkins to give us a clue about what happened to him?"

I can't think of what we could have done without taking her into our confidence, and that might be disastrous. It pains me to agree with him, but if we had a longer ride to her home or if the weather had been miserable, we might have had more time. The disappearance of Baby James is secondary after what we learned about happens to girls at that house in the eleventh month of their short, sleepy lives. "We will need help when we empty that house out," I say.

"Offer her a job when the time is right?" he asks.

Henry will be busy weaning twenty girls off of laudanum. Our ladies will have to care for thirty-five babies. I almost agree with him, but shake my head no. "She knows her employer is killing those girls. She will be reporting our conversation to Burrough tomorrow." I reach over to take Baby Edward from the nurse. Our worries can resume tomorrow. Right now, we can love this child, maybe for the first time since he was given away.

35

Sutton, the real Mr. Blackstone and I are at our usual table in the Gladstone Club. Tonight we will receive news about the person who usually occupies the empty seat. The room is decked out with Christmas cheer. The waiters know they will soon receive cash from each table, and they move about in anxious haste, careful not to drop a platter. Our man Sanders has been attentive to Sutton, making sure the martinis are just right.

Between the messages imminent arrival and my memories of all the drugged baby girls in the Burrough house, my shoulders sag with exhaustion and sadness. My tablemates banter about their petty problems, real or imagined slights and the usual political gossip. I nod, add the rehearsed remarks and push my meat and potatoes around the plate. I leave my island rum drink untouched as I know my friends will be offering whiskey with their condolences later this evening.

Sutton reminds me of the time when we attended a football match when the visiting team's fans rioted after the referee disallowed what would have been the winning goal. I am half-listening when I spot our man making a beeline for our table.

"Doctor Jekyll, you have an urgent message at the front desk," Sanders says as picks up our dinner plates.

"Excuse me, gentlemen," I say as I remove my napkin from my lap and place it on the back of my chair.

I expect to see a messenger; instead, the burly constable who accompanies Inspector Newcomen warms his hands at the fireplace. He sees me and points to the stairway. He follows me out the door to the covered entranceway, where Newcomen shifts his weight from one leg to the other. It is a bitterly cold evening. Dark clouds racing by compete with the elusive moonlight.

There is no greeting when he sees me. "It took some doing, but I located a few of your house servants from when you were a child. When your father travelled, your mother entertained different male visitors, one of them being Sir Danvers Carew."

To any other West End gentleman, such an accusation would incite furious anger. "My mother was not mentally well, and her condition worsened when my father was away," I reply. Newcomen wasn't telling me anything I didn't already know.

"When did you first know you had a half-brother?" he asks.

Of course, the house servants came across Edward Hyde when my father was away. I remain silent. No need to take the bait. The last time I insulted Newcomen, he came within an inch of shattering my skull on the lavatory floor of this fine establishment. He thinks he holds the better hand.

Filling the void of our silence, the garrulous inspector says, "As best as I can tell, Hyde went away until he was an adult and returned to London and you subsidized him. It made little sense to me how you were connected, but now it does. You provided for his welfare out of some sort of familial obligation, but you wanted nothing to do with him. That is why no one ever saw you in his company."

"Yet you think I was with him the night next to Mrs. Murphy's flat where you saw him enter a space with no other exit and saw me exit." I can't help but twist his own logic in knots. He has created what he deduces as the only plausible scenario, and I am throwing water all over it. "Did the house servants confirm what went on in the Jekyll mansion when Carew was visiting?" I ask.

"Sir Danvers Carew was an honorable man. He…"

I blurt out, "He was a sadistic pedophile. Whatever Hyde told you that morning when he spared your life was true. I never believed it until my brother recently told me Carew had done the same things to him. Did the servants remember that too?" I must have guessed right by Newcomen's expression. He has entered a battle of wits unarmed.

This lawman is not accustomed to being challenged. Edward Hyde could have driven the letter opener into his brain. He still bears the fresh cut above his Adam's apple. "Even more reason to want to interview George Jekyll. Where is he?" Newcomen is acting like a bloody bull making a fatal charge at the matador.

"In Turkey, on business. I already told you that, now if you will excuse me, I would like to return to my dinner," I say. I leave Newcomen standing on the sidewalk and am halfway up the stairs to the warm club entrance when I hear a different voice.

"Doctor Jekyll, I was sent by Attorney Utterson. This is the telegram he received within the hour."

I take the telegram and read it. I close my eyes for dramatic effect. I scan it again, pretending the words printed on it might change. "Here is your answer, Inspector Newcomen." I hand it to him with a shaky hand.

Newcomen reads, "It is with great sadness that your brother George and his business associate Edward Hyde perished at sea; there were no survivors." He reads it again silently. The import sinks in. His murder case just evaporated like morning mist on the pond in Regent's Park. He hands it back. It is from our import/export agent in Samsun, Turkey.

What Newcomen doesn't know is that Francine and I

watched George die the night Edward disappeared into the ether forever. I allow myself to grieve my brother's death in front of Newcomen while he processes the news. The elusive killer of Sir Danvers Carew, whom he has been chasing for three years, is on the bottom of the Black Sea along with my brother. At that moment, as gentlemen from the club pass Christmas tidings to each other before getting into cabs, two men drawn together by a murder no longer have a thing to say to each other.

I hand the messenger a coin and tell him, "Please tell Utterson to make funeral arrangements at St. Giles in the Fields." The messenger heads toward my barrister's abode.

"Sorry for your loss, Doctor Jekyll," he mumbles. He motions to the constable, and they walk to a waiting cab like a hunter lost in the woods. I hope he never finds his way back to me.

There will be newspaper accounts of the salvage party finding the boat, with rugs and carpets on it, in the shallows with no passengers trapped aboard. What won't be mentioned is that the elderly captain gladly accepted a princely sum to scuttle the ship and move with his family to the mountains.

Friends of George will have their funeral, and the mysterious Mr. Hyde will no longer be sought after by the raging bull Inspector Newcomen.

Hopefully, my other business with Francine and Scotland Yard with go as smoothly.

36

I am hoping Henry's plan at the club is convincing. We both know what happened to George and Edward Hyde. The longer George is absent from the London scene; more questions will arise.

Tonight, Alice and I loiter across the street from the front door of the Burrough house. She will return to the Jekyll mansion with the cab bringing Sally to Whitechapel at midnight. She is not ready to walk the streets with us yet. "Francine, I never thought I would see this place again, except in my nightmares," she says.

We are close to completing our presentation to Constable Collier and Inspector Abberline. This crucial interview with the girl's daytime nurse is all that remains. We have gotten as much as we could from the boy's daytime nurse. Celeste Pirie and the Indian doctor have told us as much as they were willing. The same goes for the chemist who supplied the doctor with unhealthy amounts of laudanum. The laundress and wet nurses gave us vital pieces of the puzzle.

We will follow the day nurse home, and Alice will question her alone. The red-haired, barren wife of the wealthy aristocrat cannot be seen with her, lest she report my presence to Mrs. Burrough. The lives of the baby girls depend on convincing the Yard men that all the deaths were not natural, before Burrough takes any drastic action. Abberline will have to move fast to make sure the witnesses provide them with the evidence to charge Burrough and the doctor.

"Maybe your nightmares will ease when you watch the girls come out of their drug-induced sleep at the New Hope Mission. Henry is paying the contractors to work round the clock to make the space ready for the nursery," I say.

"He's a good man. I've seen him around you and Lucy. He really cares for you both."

"How do you feel about Lucy staying with Henry and me if we don't find her next of kin?" I ask her pointblank.

"She's been loved by you two since the morning we pulled her out of the alley. I can't imagine anyone else giving her a better home."

I smile at her blessing. "Alice, we think you could play an important part at New Hope Mission with the nursery, with helping the babies and helping the ladies. Would you like that?"

"Do you think I am ready? I quit the last job you gave me."

"I was wrong to send you into that hellhole," I say, nodding across the street. "You fled with your sanity and didn't return to the drink. That tells me a lot about your strength of character."

She smiles. "I've always been good with babies, what's another thirty-five?"

"There she is," I whisper. Alice pulls me deeper into the shadows. I make sure my frock and hat covers all my hair. We wait until the day nurse is mid-block before we shadow her from the other side of the road. The church bells toll six times. Mrs. Burrough and Felicity have the girls all to themselves. I shiver as much at the thought as from the cold.

Edward Hyde told me how he watched over me when The Ripper was about. He had to have one eye on me and the other out for the man who sliced his forearm from elbow to wrist. He also had to worry about Inspector Newcomen and any constables who possessed a sketch of him. He went out night after night hunting The Ripper until Saucy Jack hunted me. Edward never wavered in his commitment to Henry and me to ensure our survival. It was only after he dispatched The Ripper to the afterworld, that he entrusted me to care for Henry and vanished into the ether. Henry tells me he still feels Edward's presence, but it is not outside of him, but in his heart. Edward will always be with him. The abuses he endured for Henry as child, and all of his memories came flooding back to Henry that fateful night on the docks.

"I never met her," Alice says. "She was always gone before I arrived." I follow Alice in the shadows as we remain in sight of our prey, but unlike Edward with his dagger and The Ripper with his carving tools, we are only armed with questions.

"She sat in a comfortable chair as far away as possible from the babies entering their eleventh month," I say.

Alice replies, "Aye, I know that chair. I fell asleep in it every night. What was I to do until changing time in the morning with Felicity's help?"

"She's an odd one," I say.

"She spent little time with the girls but helped the boys' night nurse when they started fussing and crying. I would wake up with the noise and go downstairs to see if they would need any help. She would pick up a boy and twirl about with him until the nurse yelled at her. "Look, did you see that?"

"Yes." The day nurse walked up the stoop of a dilapidated wooden building—three stories with lit front windows, save one.

We waited a moment and watched as the darkened window brightened.

"Good luck," I say.

Alice steps purposely under the lighting on the nearest

streetlamp. She avoids the day's horse droppings and looks back at me before entering. She returns my wave.

How long I wait depends on how much Alice can pry from this sour day nurse. I cool off from the exertion of the quick walk of nearly a mile, and I think of all the things we must do to sink Burrough and see if any clues of what happened to Baby James bob up from the deep. There is more work to be done about Celeste's suitor and his whereabouts, but now we must concentrate on saving the girls. Alice exited the building under full steam and made haste toward Commercial Street and the food stalls, where we hoped to find sustenance. I half run to catch up to her once we both turn the next corner. Alice doesn't slow down, and I wonder what was said. She crosses the next street, and cabbies yell at her to be mindful of her steps. I pick up my pace, and my longer stride make gains. Whatever happened there, Alice wants to put as much distance between the day nurse and herself. Is she now running from me? Am I going to lose her to the streets? I haven't run this fast since I was a wee one in Ireland, and my chest is pounding. A side stitch develops. I call out, "Alice."

She doesn't stop or turn. I remember how she acted when she ran straight from the Burrough house to the Jekyll manse. I press on. I can't lose her on the streets. Did I push her into some horrible revelation? "Alice, stop."

At the next intersection, she lost her bearings. In her hesitation and disorientation, I make up the gap and grasp her coat sleeve.

Terrified and hyperventilating, she collapses into my arms. We hold on to each other like we've just finished sprinting up a mountain. I catch my breath first, but Alice's color is not good, and I am afraid she is about to pass out. "We are far away from there; no one can harm us. We are safe now. We are safe." I hold her lightly. Her anxious breathing deepens. It takes all my willpower to stay calm as my mind races over all the possibilities of what the day nurse told Alice. I imagine the worst for the baby girls. What did she say to Alice that sent her flying in a panic?

She removes her tear-stained face from my shoulder. "We are all going to hang. All the nurses are going to hang if any one of us says a word to the police. I will be blamed for those two babies who didn't wake up."

37

"The sketch made all the difference," Utterson says. "The shipping agent sent his report by courier on the overnight Antwerp ferry and is standing by the telegraph office in Baarle-Hertog for further instructions."

"We promised Constable Collier he would be the first to report the identification to his superiors," I say.

Henry is seated next to me in the cab, across from his solicitor. We make tracks in the rare dusting of snow wrapping London town in a soft gauze. The factories and larger buildings belching coal soot have yet to sully the ribbons of white we travel to Scotland Yard. "And he shall, we're meeting him first before we sit down with both he and Abberline."

I fill in Utterson with all the details of Alice's meeting with the boys' day nurse. It was of such importance; she and I rode directly home. We huddled with Henry and Louise immediately upon our return and did not venture out after midnight. Utterson makes notes as best as he can as we ride over the muffled cobblestones.

Collier greets us in front of the entrance. Bright, clean sunlight illuminates him. "You have news?" he asks.

"I am well, thank you for asking." I reach out my hand, and he takes it and guides me from the carriage to the sidewalk.

"You are right, Mrs. Murphy. Where are my manners? How are you?"

"I am of two minds, Clarence. Good news about the identification of the dead girl and terrible news about dead girls at the Burrough house. We asked specifically for you to be present when we present our findings to Inspector Abberline." For Constable Collier, it is good news either way. He concludes one case (with our help) and may be included in a new investigation into the goings on at the desolate end of Whitechapel.

He ushers us into a meeting room, past suspicious inspectors probably wondering what a constable is doing with wealthy West Enders in tow. "The kettle is on. Tea?"

I prefer coffee. A new habit Henry brought home from the West Indies. Utterson nods. Collier produces two relatively clean cups and saucers.

I provide a plate and a baker's dozen of shortbreads from my small basket. "From New Hope Mission Bakery," I say.

Once settled with tea and shortbread, "We have a name for the girl, then?" His excitement is palpable.

Utterson produces a sheaf of papers. "The Jekyll Import & Export shipping agent made his reports out to you. When he had no luck at the ports of entry here, he scoured the ports across the Channel as far up as Antwerp. Your lead of the girl's shoes being made in Holland landed him there."

"But it was the sketch you ordered two copies of that made a difference. A young sailor recognized her and assisted her on the gangplank and helped her when she became seasick during the crossing," I say.

"She arrived in London a week before the night she died. Where she stayed is still a mystery," Henry says.

"And the piece of paper with the foundling house address?" Collier asks after inhaling his second shortbread.

The three of us look at each other and with our eyes elect Utterson to answer. "It may tie into the larger inquiry we would ask you and Inspector Abberline to undertake. Don't be surprised if the girl had gone to that house, was sent away and got lost on the streets of Whitechapel."

"I am not surprised at all. Remember, I met Mrs. Burrough," he says.

"We know she had luggage, two carryalls and a purse," Henry says.

"She had no possessions when we found her," Collier adds.

"The back of her coat and skirt were sullied from the birth, but otherwise her clothes were clean," I say. My experience with the ladies of the evening has made me observant in this matter. When they appear on the streets in the same clothes they wore the night before and previous nights, I know they are at their lowest. Sleeping rough and trading sex for gin is where I find women who cannot sink any lower. Sally and I ply them with sweets, water and promise of a warm bed, bath and clean clothes, but it is their decision to leave this life which begins their new one.

"Aye, but do you think they have been confiscated and sold for not paying for her rooms?" Collier asks.

"There may be correspondence in her possessions between her and Mrs. Burrough which may explain why she was going there," Utterson adds.

"My ladies know every doss house and flophouse on that side of the river. It would take us but a day to sort that out," I say.

"Especially having the girl's name," Utterson says.

Collier turns to the second to last page of the report. It contains notes taken from a baptism certificate from the village where she was born. "Hanne Herbeit, born August 13, 1872." He looks to the ceiling and ciphers out her age. "Barely sixteen at the time of death. Pregnant at fifteen." He points to the parents' names. "Are they still alive?"

Utterson clears his throat. "Yes, the father identified her from the sketch. The mother was hysterical." He points to the last page.

"Do they want to claim the body?" Collier asks.

"They are poor people and…" Utterson stops.

"The father sent her away. She hid her pregnancy as long as she could," I say. "Let me ask you, which is better, living a lifetime of shame of having your unwed daughter give birth or the regret of sending your child away when she needed you the most and having her die in an alley giving birth, all alone?" I became angry when Utterson told me that earlier in the cab. The men at the table hear it in my voice now.

Collier put down the last of his third shortbread. Henry set down his cuppa. None of the men made eye contact with me.

"They will not come forward to claim the body. I will have them sign an affidavit to that effect." Utterson says.

"And the baby?" Collier asks.

Inspector Abberline opens the to door to the meeting room and greets us. "Sorry for my tardiness." He sighs. "The newspapers are saying The Ripper is one of the Royals and that we are protecting him."

The strain on his face is apparent. Only time will let The Ripper slip into history. I know why Whitechapel is safe from that monster, but the added patrols and better treatment of the ladies of the night is a benefit the Metropolitan Police would not provide otherwise. Henry and I know the Ripper's true identity and, for good reasons, have sworn ourselves to secrecy. Yet, here we sit, about to tell Abberline of a killer who has been operating behind closed doors for over a decade.

38

Constable Clarence Collier is about to make the most important presentation of facts and assumptions to a superior officer he has ever undertaken, and if it goes well for him, inclusion on the team of investigators would be the most likely outcome. He introduces us and reminds Abberline of how my suggestions assisted his investigation. Witnesses provided different two sketches of The Ripper. One was spot on and the other was of Edward Hyde. My conversations with Abberline have always had an important motive. He listened to my suggestions without scoffing when I also gave him my reasons.

But first, Collier must share the good news. "We found the dead girl's parents, and they identified her from the sketch and how far along she was with child. Her name is Hanne Herbiet from Belgium. She was sixteen at the time of death and did not have a husband. I will have the affidavit shortly from her parents not wishing to claim the body."

Abberline nodded. "And the scrap of paper with the address of that foundling house at the far end of Whitechapel where Mrs. Murphy's nephew went missing?"

I am impressed with his memory. While being in charge of

the investigation into London's most heinous butchery for the entire autumn, he didn't miss the facts tying these two cases together. "The connection hasn't been made yet, but there is much more at stake. I commissioned Mrs. Murphy and Doctor Jekyll to go undercover with the help of their employee Alice Hardy to penetrate the foundling house run by Mrs. Burrough. Events have galloped. I haven't had a chance to give you an interim report. I am asking them to report. Better to hear it from their lips than hearsay from me. You can ask them questions directly, as time is of the essence."

I never underestimated Constable Collier, but how he just handled being in the dark since the day we pretended to know him from vestry at Trinity Paddington was elegant.

Abberline looks at me. "Mrs. Murphy, undercover?"

"Caroline, the wife of wealthy Edward Blackwell. They just adopted a boy from Mrs. Burrough and are about to rescue a girl from that horrid house."

"Alice Hardy replaced the night nurse who tended to the girls until two allegedly died in their sleep one night. She also supplied us with information as late as last night about the missing boy," Henry says.

"Thanks to Alice, we found a former laundress who told us about wet nurses who came and went there. They told us about the girl Alice replaced, Celeste Pirie, and her beau, Archie Rathbone, who visited her overnight," I say.

"Doctor Jekyll used his medical training to find a chemist who identified the physician who pronounced those two girls dead of heart disease from natural causes," Collier says. I am glad I gave him the broad outline in order to set up this meeting.

Utterson says, "Those are the people central to this inquiry. Alice ran away from that house as fast as she could. Doctor Jekyll and Mrs. Murphy played their roles to the end of the second act. As the curtain rises on the third act, this is where Inspector Frederick Abberline and Constable Clarence Collier brings the end to this tragedy by using all their authority to compel truthful answers."

"It's a sordid business Burrough conducts, sir," Collier sets up Utterson for the explanation.

On cue, Utterson begins his monologue. "As best we can tell, Mr. Burrough left Mrs. Burrough shortly after he realized their only daughter was touched. She kept the house and began advertising a baby service where mothers would pay her to care for their infants while they got their affairs straightened out. They enter into a contract with her to care for their babies for a set period, usually a year. After that time, if they do not return for their children, she is free to make them available for adoption."

"That was the deal Rosie O'Sullivan had with Mrs. Burrough for my nephew," I say.

"Except he went missing," Abberline says.

I nod, but Utterson continues, "She makes her money on both ends with the boys by taking them in for a fee and taking an adoption fee from couples like the couple Mrs. Murphy and Doctor Jekyll pretended to be."

"And none of the women return for their children," Abberline asks.

"None, sir," Collier responds. "But it is about the girls that we are meeting today."

Utterson continues, "We are told there is very little market for infant girls. Burrough will try to add one when a couple selects a boy, but it is rare. There are no takers for the girls, and when their contract expires..."

"So do they," Henry says.

"Come again," Abberline stutters.

"That's what I said, Guv," Collier adds for effect.

I say, "None of the mothers return for their babies, Burrough has no money to care for them after the contract. She can adopt out the boys but not most of the girls."

"So she kills them off before the contracts expire, usually before they turn one year old," Utterson says.

"How?" Abberline understands the enormity of what is being discussed and leans in on both elbows.

"Overdoses of laudanum," Henry says. "The girls are sedated from the time they are old enough to take a bottle, and when the time comes, she gives them twice as much. They die overnight. The chemist said he delivers enough laudanum to the doctor to tranquillize a stable of horses."

"How many girls?" Abberline asks.

Utterson says, "We copied twenty-nine death certificates of girls dying of natural causes from heart disease." He produces a folder and hands it to Collier, who is seeing it for the first time but was told about it.

"Twice as many didn't make it that long, according to death certificates of girls at that location, all signed off by the same doctor," Henry says as Utterson passes over a second thicker file. "They are underfed, diluted goat's milk, and kept in a sleep state almost twenty-fours a day. They die from malnutrition or failure to thrive, but the doctor finds other causes and manners of death to list. I've been in those rooms twice. The first time, I didn't know what I was looking at, and the second time I did."

"The girls pay for the general upkeep of the house while the boys generate a profit. It's a rotten business," Collier repeats what I told him a day before. Excellent memory.

"And the missing boy?" Abberline asks.

"There are missing links in what the witnesses told us," I say. "But last night Alice Hardy talked to the boy's day nurse, who came in the morning the boy was found missing. She thought nothing was amiss until Rosie O'Sullivan came back with her last payment and it became apparent the boy was truly missing.

Mrs. Burrough summoned her daughter, who told her about Archie Rathbone and Celeste Pirie and how Archie held the baby boy while the night nurse was asleep, saying how he would like one for his own. According to the boys' day nurse, before Rosie reported James missing, Mrs. Burrough summoned Celeste, and Celeste brought in Archie. She sent Celeste home. Archie and Mrs. Burrough had a terrible row behind closed doors. The day nurse thinks Archie turned the tables on her and threatened to tell the police about what was happening to the girls."

"Then what?" Collier asks.

Utterson says, "That's where the trail turns cold. Archie fled his home after collecting his last paycheck that day and hasn't been seen since."

"He extorted her, and she paid him," Abberline says.

"That's our current theory," Utterson says.

"And the boy?" Collier asks.

"Took the boy for his own buyer," I say.

"Find Archie and find out who he sold James to," Collier says.

"But in the meantime, there is the matter of the girls," Abberline says.

"The wealthy couple arranged with Mrs. Burrough to take a girl. We chose the one with the least amount of time before her contract expired. Burrough said she needed to complete the adoption with the birth mother because the contract hadn't expired yet, but I know it is to wean the girl off of the laudanum," Henry says. "I can do that the minute we remove her from that vile place. Each of the other girls in that room furthest from the back stairway are in immediate danger."

Utterson hands Collier eight more files. "These are the memoranda of interviews of the laundress, wet nurses, house nurses, chemist and attending physician with all their addresses and what questions remain for each one."

"If you're right about all this, she's a stone-cold killer and has been operating behind closed doors for years."

"Nobody cares about the babies," I say.

"Throwaway children," Collier says.

"That's cold," I retort.

"Doesn't make it any less true," he says. "Your sister-in-law came back with her money and to say her last goodbyes."

"I cannot disagree with you, Clarence," I say. "Since I found out what Burrough was really doing, I thanked the heavens it wasn't a girl."

"Although she might have still been there and you would have never been called in to help," Abberline astutely points out.

"And then six or seven months from now, your husband would be notified of the baby's unfortunate death. He would be sad but none the wiser," Collier says. He'll make a good detective someday, stuffing his emotions the way I have to in order to get the job done.

"I will take this immediately to the Superintendent. I need more manpower," Abberline says.

"I volunteer to go with you when you interview the chemist and the doctor. My expertise might come in handy. Besides, the chemist likes me, and the doctor fears me."

That raises eyebrows among the Yard men.

"The nurses who still work there have been threatened into silence by Burrough. She will try to say the girls' nurse drugged them to keep them quiet," I say.

"One last thing, gentlemen," Henry says. "Since we learned about what Burrough was doing, I have built a space where we can care for all the babies. We will have Alice Hardy in charge of the nursery and wet nurses on call twenty-four hours. I will act as the physician to wean the girls off the drugs, and we will have all manner baby clothes and a laundry set up in time for their removal from the Foundling House. We have a solution for you when the time is ready."

"New Hope Mission?" Abberline asks.

"Seems I will be busier than ever, Inspector," I say as I stand. Collier gets to his feet, as does Henry. The meeting has come to a close. I am pleased with the way we made our presentation. I have garnered the trust of Inspector Abberline and have nurtured relationships with both him and Collier.

Utterson remains seated. "A private matter for Inspector Abberline, if I may."

"Is it brief?" Abberline asks and sits back down.

Utterson nods. He will implore Abberline to make sure Newcomen is nowhere near this investigation and explain why.

The door closes behind us. Collier reiterates his grave concerns for the children, but beneath that professional mantle beats the heart of a young man on a chase.

39

"I figured you would be back," the chemist says to me.

"I am Doctor Henry Jekyll, and this is Constable Collier," I say. The snow melted in the brilliant mid-December sunshine, and by late afternoon Abberline and Collier, with a phalanx of uniformed constables, arrived at my home. He had received permission to begin the investigation. We split up. Abberline, Francine and the constables headed to the foundling house.

"I asked my bookkeeper to pull all the records for Doctor Meherhomji going back three years. Here are the receipts. We copied the ledger pages for his account." He lifted the ledger onto the counter and opened it. A second later, a bulging stack of receipts appeared.

"How can I compensate you for your time?" I ask him.

His gaze shifted from me to Collier. "Keep my business out of the newspapers. I always wondered what he was doing with all that laudanum, but it wasn't until you came along, Doctor, I put it together. If I had known what he was doing, I would never have sold him a single remedy."

"It's not my decision to make, but I can make the recommendation if what you are saying is true, but if I catch you lying to us once, I will see to it you are charged with accessory to murder."

The chemist, tall, thin, older with patchy grey hair, bobbed his head in agreement. "At first I thought he needed it for treating hysterical women, but his other requests didn't seem to be for the female population. He later confided in me that he had been visiting multiple foundling houses and had been treating infants."

"What ailment requires this remedy for infants?" Collier asks me.

"Answer him," I say to the chemist, who is tapping the counter nervously.

"Teething, colic, generalized upset. They pack the houses with babies, and one baby crying sets off the entire room; none of the infants would get any sleep, and that would set up a whole cascade of problems."

"Given the amount of laudanum you were providing him, how many infants would you say he was treating?" I ask.

"That would be hard to calculate."

Collier reaches into the stack and pulls out a random month. "Here is one month."

"Divide the total by the appropriate infant dose and again by the usual amount of doses per child."

"Each child would be different because of age, weight and other factors," the chemist replies.

"Use an average," I say with the right amount of exasperation in my voice.

Collier scans the remaining receipts as the chemist takes pencil to paper. The minutes tick by whilst I peruse the ledger. I have some questions for the chemist when he finishes his ciphers.

Collier mutters, "Meherhomji is ordering almost nothing other than laudanum."

"He must see an awful amount of sickly infants," the chemist says after during the totaling.

I glance at Collier, who nods. We weren't sure the chemist was in on the scheme, and by making him do the numbers we are getting the idea he wasn't.

"Why do you say that?" Collier asks.

"One moment," he says. We see him completing the long division. "Assuming he see hundreds of children every week, he only needs to administer to a percentage who are sick with maladies requiring laudanum."

"And there is no record of other remedies for infants with other symptoms," Collier says.

"You're correct," the chemist says without looking up from his sums.

I exchange glances with the policeman. The chemist is about to find out what Meherhomji was doing, and we want to see his honest reaction.

"One hundred and fifty infants are receiving the average dose the recommended number of times for those symptoms during a course of a month." He sighs and puts down his pencil.

"Thirty-five to fifty children in a house," I say.

"How many houses with babies suffering as you stated would he be visiting?"

"Too many," the chemist says.

"Estimate," Collier retorts.

"On the low side, fifteen houses." The chemist clears his throat. "That's an estimate."

Collier says, "Doctor Meherhomji only visits one foundling house regularly."

The look of confusion is obvious and immediate. "How is that possible?" He turns the ledger around and shakes his head. He paws through the stack of receipts. "That's not possible."

"And from that house he only prescribes to twenty girls," I say.

He utters, "Twenty sick girls?"

"No," Collier says. "All twenty girls every day."

The chemist gulps. He looks at his sums. He scans the ledger and pushes the receipts away from him like they are poison.

We take the ledger and the passel of receipts. We have our answer.

COLLIER AND I hear the weary footsteps of a person dragging a bad leg up stairs. The person moves slowly with labored breath. We are on the landing just below the floor where Meherhomji lives. The title of doctor for this man will never pass my lips.

The stairway is dimly lit, and Collier calls to the man as he turns the corner and faces us. "I am Clarence Collier from Scotland Yard. You are under arrest for aiding Mrs. Burrough's murder of infant girls."

"I have done nothing wrong. I never administered a single dose. Mrs. Burrough was given explicit instructions about what to do when a girl was sick. I am innocent." It sounds like he has been rehearsing those lines, and it isn't for West End theatre.

Collier moves to secure him in irons. As he goes behind him, he offers no resistance. Meherhomji sees me, and his eyes widen. "That man threatened to beat me with a poker."

"Did he throw you down several flights of stairs?" Collier whips him around and holds his arms taut and has Meherhomji teetering on the landing facing the stairs.

"No," he shrieks.

Collier says, "We know what happened when a girl outlived her time there. Tell us about the others who died."

"I don't know what you are talking about." He pushes back with his good leg.

Collier pulls his arms higher behind his back and says, "You are going to Scotland Yard with us now. I won't ask you again."

I flash back to Newcomen's rough treatment of me over trying to find Hyde, and I place a hand on Collier's shoulder. As much as I hate what Newcomen did to me, I won't watch Meherhomji 'accidentally fall down the stairs when he tries to run away from us.' Especially if he accidentally falls down every flight of stairs. "And every nurse will testify in your defense; they never saw you give the girls laudanum?" I ask.

"Yes!"

"And you will tell us how you treated any of the boys who were sick?" I ask.

"Yes!"

"And how the only times you went to the girls" floor was to pronounce them dead?" I ask.

"Yes!"

"Did you find it strange that most of the boys lived and most of the girls didn't?"

"Yes!"

"The boys were treated differently from the girls."

Collier reasserted his hold on the man he had just arrested.

"Yes!"

"Was it a miracle any of the girls survived as long as some of them did?"

He was crying now. As his shoulders heaved, it caused him to compensate by trying to stand taller on his good leg. "Yes."

"And you will put this all in a statement when we get to Scotland Yard?" Collier asks.

A defeated yes emits from his lips. He is shaking now.

I feel Collier lower the physician's arms and pull him back from what would have been a nasty trip and fall. We take him by both arms and walk him down each flight of stairs to the sidewalk. Darkness had set in while we had waited for him to come home. Collier blows out three long bleats on his whistle, and within a minute a cab arrives. We put our arrestee in the cab and stand with our backs and voices away from our ride.

"Utterson told us the laws regarding Meherhomji's negligence are vague unless someone saw him do something directly to one of the babies," Collier says.

"Farm animals are better protected," I say.

"You know an inspector will take over the interviewing when we get him into a room," he says.

"I will insist you be present too, Clarence, unless Abberline needs you for a more important task."

"That works," he said. "Given how much laudanum the chemist provided Meherhomji and if he says he supplied all of it to Burrough…"

"And he admits to us, he saw none of the boys look as lifeless as the girls…"

Collier is spot on with the line of questioning. "And the boys' nurses never left Burrough alone with the boys…"

"The chemist and another well-respected doctor can say that with the amount of laudanum each girl was given, survival 'til eleven months old would have been a miracle. Meherhomji knew what he was doing when he gave her the drugs." I finish our train of thought.

4 0

"What is the meaning of this?" Mrs. Burrough tries to stem the flood of blue serge coated constables through the foyer.

Felicity runs to the backstairs. The nursery rhyme emitted from her trembling lips is hushed. She looks confused, not knowing whether to run upstairs to her room or to the basement. "I want my dolly," she says as her bare feet slap down the stairs.

A second wave comes through the front door. These are the women from New Hope Mission. Alice leads them in. She points up the central stairway. "Boys on the second floor, girls on the third," she says.

"You can't go up there," Burrough crosses her arms in defiance.

"Baby killer," Alice pushes past her with a vicious shove.

"It's over, Mrs. Burrough," Abberline says. "Show us where you keep the laudanum."

"I will do no such thing," she says. It takes a moment, but she recognizes me "What are you doing here?"

"I am Francine Murphy, and you are going to tell me where James O'Sullivan is."

"I told the police before. He went missing, and I don't know who took him. If that is what you have invaded my house for, the answer is the same."

"If you don't tell us where you keep the laudanum, I will have my men tear your house apart." Abberline barks at her.

The day nurses are led downstairs by two constables each and are paraded past Burrough. We hear one constable say, "We will sort it all out at Scotland Yard."

"Remember what I said," Burrough yells to them as they are escorted to waiting cabs.

"This search warrant is signed by a magistrate for the laudanum. Last chance to cooperate," Abberline says.

The next group of women entering are the wet nurses. Behind them, two befuddled physicians, who Henry shanghaied from his club on short notice.

"Third floor," I say. "The girls are first."

"What do you think you are doing?" Burrough screeches.

Abberline moves with a quickness he might have needed in his constable days to break up a bar fight and grabs her arm. "You are coming with me." He fast-walks her to the kitchen opposite the office and forces her into a chair. "Don't get up."

I hear, "Doctor Jekyll sent me here, said I might be of help." I don't recognize the trembling, older, grey-haired man.

"And who might you be?" I ask.

"The chemist who sold the laudanum to Dr. Meherhomji."

"Go with them and describe to them what they are looking for." I point to the remaining two constables. When he departs, I close the door to the kitchen, and the cacophony of babies crying is muffled. Abberline is seated next to Mrs. Burrough, and I am across the table from her. It's a good thing, too; otherwise, I might be tempted to slap her hard. She looks to be having trouble breathing. The corseted teal dress with the ramrod straight backing is constricting her lungs.

"A very pregnant blonde sixteen-year-old from Holland came here early last week. Her name is Hanne Herbeit; She died giving childbirth near to here. Why did you send her away?" I ask. I make a presumption and expect a denial.

"Who are you to dare to talk to me? You lied about who you were to get a baby boy. You and that man bargained with me like I was selling day-old bread in the market."

"Mrs. Murphy consults with Scotland Yard from time to time. She has been of great assistance in the Ripper matter."

"Murphy, the do-gooder?"

"Yes," Abberline says. "Now answer her question."

"I told her to come back after she had the baby, and I would see if we would accept it."

"Did she have a purse when you talked to her?" Abberline asks.

"Why yes, she reached into it to show me she had the money for us to care for it while she got situated."

"Did she tell where she was staying?"

"No, but I didn't think it was far away. In her condition, she couldn't walk very far; her feet were swollen. Those shoes looked like they were cutting into her skin."

"She had a healthy girl," I say. "How would that have changed your arrangements?" Getting Burrough to talk about something that didn't affect her would hopefully loosen her lips for talking about the goings-on in this abominable house of horrors.

"Same fee to board her girl for a year, ten pounds."

"How many mothers returned to claim their babies when the time came?" Abberline asked.

"Most did," she lied.

Abberline stands and looks down at her. "Show us your records."

"Those are private matters between me and my clients; I will do no such thing." Her breathing becomes ragged again.

"Mrs. Burrough." He reaches into his coat pocket. "I have a court order to remove all the babies from this house. Your business is over. What do you think the wet nurses, nurses and doctors are here for? They are getting the infants ready for travel.

"Not the boys; they all have adoption contracts!"

"And the girls?" I ask.

"Their mothers will come back for them," Burrough falsely explains. She has it all figured out. Adoption service for the boys, boarding service for the girls. Except for one thing. The girls never reunite with their mothers.

"It's over, Mrs. Burrough. You're finished. Do you have someone to care for Felicity?" Abberline asks.

"How do you know her name?" Burrough spits out her question like an accusation.

"Take your pick, Mrs. Burrough. The laundress you stopped paying, the wet nurses, Celeste Pirie, Alice Hardy, shall I go on?" he asks.

The kitchen door bursts open. A constable holding a simple glass flask with an amber liquid says, "Found it." The chemist nods behind him.

Mrs. Burrough tries to lunge at it and large firm hand pushes her back down. "This is how you killed the oldest girls and kept the rest drugged in a stupor," Abberline delivers the accusation.

"No, I supplied the nurses with the correct formulas; they must have increased the dosages to keep the girls asleep."

"And kill some?" I stand and lean over the table.

"I know nothing about that." She tries to stand up again, and the tightness of her dress and the accusation of murder causes her to faint.

Felicity carries a rag doll into the kitchen, followed by Alice.

She sees her mother tilted against the sideboard. To the casual observer, she appears asleep.

"Mary, Mary, quite contrary. How does your garden grow? With silver bells, and cockle shells,

and pretty maids all in a row. And pretty maids all in a row. And pretty maids all in a row."

Alice gathers her into her arms. "Odd, she's been singing this rhyme since we arrived."

"What's odd about it?" I ask.

"I never recalled her singing this song before," Alice replies.

"Felicity Burrough, what are you trying to tell us?" I ask.

She points towards her mother. "Mary, Mary, quite contrary. How does your garden grow? With silver bells and cockle shells and pretty maids all in a row. Pretty maids all in a row, Pretty maids all in a row."

"Inspector Abberline," I say. My head is swimming. I am feeling faint as well. The realization of what this imp has been saying. We never paid attention to the nattering of a child who was touched in the head. I lift my right hand and point through the kitchen window towards the rear of the house. "The garden, pretty maids all in a row."

———

THE CHURCH BELLS TOLL MIDNIGHT. I lost count of the constables arriving with shovels and torches. The entire garden is lit by torches mounted on poles. At eight, Louise took Felicity Burrough for safekeeping. The poor girl was inconsolable when she was removed from the premises. The coroner arrived shortly after ten, went to the garden, surveyed the ghastly scene and rushed past me to the loo and threw up.

At one point all the digging stopped at past eleven. A few minutes ago, Celeste Pirie was brought from Scotland Yard back to the house where she had worked as the girls' night nurse. She was led to the garden. From the kitchen window, I watched them lead her through a maze of poles with flags. There are too many flags to count. Each represents a grave. A few are boys, but none of the boys appear to be recently buried, I am told. They haven't found a new grave for any boy, especially one with a birthmark behind the left ear. I am exhausted, but I dare not fall asleep.

Celeste cries out from the garden, "Archie!"

41

Mary Burrough sits on a couch in her office with a blank stare on her face. A solemn constable stands between her and the doorway. All the babies have been removed to New Hope Mission. She refuses to answer questions while Abberline and Collier pore over her records. I came straightaway when word of the discoveries in garden reached Scotland Yard. We were finishing up with Meherhomji when the news broke like a tidal wave. I've never seen Francine so utterly shattered. She melted into my arms, muttering, "All those babies."

The house is ungodly quiet.

I immediately stiffen when I hear a voice I recognize. It is Newcomen. He walks towards Abberline. "Some graves have more than one body. I've told the men to dig deeper after we remove the first body."

We make eye contact. Utterson's warning worked for the initial stages of the foundling house investigation, but that baby went out with the bathwater when it was learned what was planted in the garden.

"Doctor Jekyll, Mrs. Murphy." He tips his bowler.

"Inspector Newcomen." I return the greeting. Usually, Hyde's ethereal presence warns me when danger is lurking, but not now. The amount of death and misery on these grounds is oppressive and overwhelming. There are scant words to describe what has been uncovered here, both literally and figuratively. The total number of girls buried in the garden far exceeds the number of death certificates on file. The number of autopsies will not rival the sinking of the Princess Alice a decade earlier, but just the same, the total will be staggering.

We are seated on the other well-worn leather couch in the room. I whisper into Francine's ear, "There is not much more here we need to learn about the baby girls. When they count the number of girls out in the graves, they should have a realistic number. More importantly, we removed all the babies."

"Why did Burrough murder Archie Rathbone?" she whispers back. "We know they argued."

"I hear you whispering about me over there," Burrough hisses at us.

Newcomen stops by the office door; Abberline and Collier look up from the ledgers.

Abberline says, "Francine, do you have something to say to Mrs. Burrough?"

"As a matter of fact, I do. The boys' day nurse overheard you arguing with Archie Rathbone. He disappeared the following day. Celeste Pirie just identified his body in your garden. He head was caved in."

Coming out of her trance, Burrough says, "And you think I killed him. You think I killed all those babies. You think I am a monster. Did you ever stop to consider that those mothers who came here never wanted to see their babies again? Did you ever stop to consider what their lives would have been like if they had remained with their mothers? Ask the policemen how many babies wash up at low tide on the Thames.

"When my sister-in-law Rosie O'Sullivan set sail for America, she never intended to return for Baby James, but she probably expected him to be adopted out to an excellent family," Francine replies.

Mary Burrough shakes her head. "That child is the cause of all this. All this." She waves her arm in a wide circle.

"Pray tell," I say.

"That boy Archie told me he knew what happened to that baby, but he would only tell me if I paid him. He gave me a price. I said I needed a day to get the money together. I told your sister-in-law to come back the day after we discovered the boy missing, and I would have the answer for her then."

No one says anything to her. I hope no one bursts into the room with another grisly finding. The silence drags with all eyes on her. Somewhere a clock chimes once. The old house creaks under the weight of untold horrors.

"The next day, he came back and tried to renegotiate. I wanted to kill him. I did want to kill him. I stood firm. The little shit was trying to bully me while he was extorting me. He realized I had no more money to give him. I gave him half. He said he would show me. We walked to the back stairway, and he turned to go down the steps that's when...."

"It's okay, I think I know what you are going to say," Francine nods at her to finish her sentence.

"You can't prosecute her anyway; she's an imbecile. She is child."

"It was Felicity who killed Archie," Francine says.

"Stove his head in with a coal shovel. He was dead before he hit the basement floor."

"So what about the baby?" I ask.

"The bastard could have told me, but no, he had to be a show off. I hid his body until nighttime and dragged him back to the garden. The secret died with him. Your sister-in-law came back that afternoon, and when I didn't produce the boy who she was going to give up, she contacted the police."

"And she got me, I mean us, involved." Francine reaches for my hand and clenches it.

"And now this." Mary Burrough falls back onto the couch, and for the first time, shows sadness. I am not sure there is any remorse, only the feelings of what is going to happen to her now. Like the cab driver who tramples a running child not caring a wit about the lad, but only what it might do to his livelihood.

Abberline harrumphs. "The nurses killed the girls, and your half-wit daughter killed Archie. How convenient. You didn't kill anybody."

Through covered eyes, Burrough says, "I didn't kill the extortionist."

We wait in silence again. Clock ticking, with the sounds of metal spades striking garden stones outside. There are over one hundred graves in the garden, and she says she is not even responsible for the one full-size body found next to the frost-bitten marigolds.

My arm shivers right where The Ripper cut Edward from elbow to wrist. A sensation emanates from gut to my chest and I pant with shallow breaths. Will Edward transform in front of Newcomen and the others? I shake. Felicity, coal shovel. Head stove in. She had to be behind and above him to do that. Archie would show Burrough. He would show her.

I look at Newcomen. He is staring at me. He's been chasing Edward for three years. He must be feeling Edward's presence.

Francine asks, "Henry?"

She senses something's amiss. She has seen Hyde transform into Jekyll. Is she about to see Jekyll transform into Hyde? Will the killer of Carew make his appearance once and for all, especially in front of the man hunting him?

I stare back at Newcomen. It feels like our minds are working at high speed to make sense of what clues Burrough has just supplied us. His mind and my mind melding.

Together, Newcomen and I say, "The basement."

"Has anyone checked the basement?" Collier asks.

Francine is right behind Newcomen as they race down the steps. I am right behind them with Collier and Abberline bringing up the rear.

42

It has been over two weeks since he went missing. Could Baby James still be alive? Felicity would know how to care for him. Fresh clothes from the laundry. Leftover bottles of cow's milk for the boys. He is down here. We use lit matches until lanterns are brought from the work in the garden. The coal furnace was stoked before our arrival and emitted heat and a soft glow from the back of the basement. Discarded furniture is piled helter-skelter across one side. The men are better suited for moving them around; I paw through the discarded boxes. Mr. Burrough was a haberdasher specializing in ladies' hats.

"Empty this basement of anything that is not nailed down," Abberline barks. A bucket brigade of constables forms on the steps. Chairs, broken desks and cribs are hoisted from the basement up the backstairs and thrown into the parlor. A large armoire has to be lifted by two men. The constable walking backward trips on the uneven ground, and the contents from the side drawers cascade onto him. Our attention is drawn to the trip, but he screams like he is being attacked by rats. He rolls away and points to the dirt floor from his knees. "Look!"

Immediately, we converge in a semi-circle around him. Our

lanterns threw off light in a kaleidoscope fashion. There appears to be several lifelike dolls on the ground. As the lighting settles into a yellowish wash, Henry says, "These are mummified babies."

The armoire is immediately righted, and Abberline opens each side door from the bottom up. "Here's one." The next one is empty. "Here's another." There is one more drawer that hadn't spilled open. He looks inside and nods his head. "Two more in here."

"They are all boys," Collier says, knelling over the ones that fell onto the unsuspecting constable, who is gagging back vomit.

Stupefied, I turn with my lantern and walk to the furthest point away from the stairs. This is where I would keep a crying baby, so the noise wouldn't reach the first floor. Felicity wanted a baby of her own. She was still a child underneath the exterior of a prepubescent girl.

I hear a faint cry. "Quiet!" I scream. Movement and voices in the basement ceases. The coal furnace groans back at me from the opposite side of the space. Footsteps above creak the floorboards. This time I hear a whimper coming from a chest of drawers. Like Abberline, I start at the bottom drawer. Baby clothes. They smell fresh and clean. I run my free hand over all four corners. Next drawer contains baby blankets. Nice quality. Next drawer, which would be at waist height for Felicity, is cracked open an inch. I bend down, feel warmth from the opening wash over my cheeks.

I open it, and what I see takes my breath away. "Henry," I call out. He appears over my shoulder and adjusts his lantern to bathe the interior in light.

The baby squints at us and rustles. I set my lantern down and lift the infant from the makeshift crib. I lift the child onto my shoulder. "Is it him?"

Henry holds the lantern to better illuminate the back of the baby's head. He is looking for a birthmark behind the left ear. It all comes down to this moment. All the subterfuge. All the foot slogging to find the women who worked here. The promise Mary McCreary and I made to Rosie. Every moment taken away from my original mission with New Hope. I scan Henry's face for the first hint. He smiles.

"Say hello to James O'Sullivan," Henry announces.

Cheers erupt from the men assembled in the basement. For one moment, they can celebrate a joyous discovery amid all the death in this dank room.

Henry and I cradle the baby between us in a warm embrace. I sob. Tears, equal parts joy and relief, fall on the infant's black hair.

We soon realize he needs changing. While I remove the wet nappy and dry him off, Henry does a cursory inspection. "I won't know better until I can examine him in my surgery, but he looks healthy." No rashes, and his breathing is normal. I pull the dry and expensive baby clothes from the lower drawer and dress James.

We carefully walk him out of the basement and into the parlor. There, Mary Burrough looks up and sees us. "You found him?"

I nod.

"You never suspected your daughter of taking him?" Abberline shouts from the stairway entrance.

She looks into her hands and says, "She was always going on and on about her dollies. I thought she was talking about those stupid rag things she carried about."

"Come here, Mrs. Burrough," Abberline commands. "I want to show you something."

Henry and I are out the front door and down the steps onto the street, where we once stood with Constable Clarence Collier, where we hatched our plan before meeting Burrough for the first time and where we decided to adopt. The morning is still, with no wind to speak of, not a cloud in the sky. Stars, like angels, too numerous to count, stretch across the expanse of the heavens.

Her screams emanating from the basement pierce the night. She never knew about other missing babies until that moment. How could that be? Were they just things to her to be counted like inventory?

Henry held James until I got settled in the cab and handed him to me. "Rosemary Lane," I say to the driver. As we drive away from Henry, his confused look begs to know why I am going directly to Seamus Murphy.

43

As soon as the cab departed the foundling house, my senses took over. I direct the driver to take me to the nearest wet nurse I know. James is in need, no telling the last time he was fed. Betsy Dyer is willing after I press coins into her palm. Back in the cab with the baby, we bounce and jostle to McCreary's. This is an interrupted night's sleep Mary will remember for the rest of her life. I rap hard on the door, and a sleepy Gabby spots me through the front plate-glass window.

"Tell your mother to dress warmly; it is cold out here."

Her eyes widen, and she points to the face popping out of the swaddling clothes.

"It's our secret, now scoot," I say.

I wait on the sidewalk between the carriage and the store. The horse is warm, and I hold James between myself and her. She eyes my prize, and I can only imagine what the mare is thinking. Something about mothers and babies, I suppose.

"What is so damn important, Francine? You drag me out of a warm bed into the dead of night and swear my daughter to secrecy," Mary says. She cannot see the bundle I am holding.

I turn, "James O'Sullivan, say hello to your Aunt Mary."

Mary McCreary has had many surprises in her life. Most of them didn't end well, but not this one. I have successfully made her the happiest woman in Whitechapel at that darkest moment before the dawn. She rushes me and throws her arms around me and twirls me to put James in a better light. "He's beautiful. Oh, Francine, you did it."

"No, we did it, Henry, Utterson, and all the ladies of New Hope Mission and all the men in Scotland Yard, made it possible. No time to waste; come with me. We are going to pay Seamus a visit. Lots to tell."

———

Newcomen and I share a pleasant goodbye. I doubt this will be the last time I speak with him, but our terms of engagement have changed forever. He and I know what happened in the parlor. Hyde was the common link fusing our thoughts to arrive at the same conclusion. He had been chasing that killer for three years and tried to get into Hyde's mind to figure out what his next move would be. Hyde has been with me since I was five years old and in some fashion remains deep in my tissues and psyche. Who would have thought that our connections to Hyde would lead to finding James O'Sullivan?

They no longer need a doctor on site. There are no more living babies to assess. The enormity of this tragedy is sinking in, but other thoughts are crowding it out as I walk to New Hope Mission. They might need me there as they settle thirty-five infants, twenty of whom have to be weaned from laudanum. I trust Alice and Louise will have everything under control. Sally is probably back in the kitchen baking enough bread and treats to feed an army. My thoughts drift to Lucy, Baby Edward, and Lucky at the mansion on Cavendish Square. What will happen to them?

I had shut down my feelings after seeing Francine ride off

to see Seamus. What will she do? What will become of us? Those questions bubble up feelings of significant loss and finality. As long as we were looking for Rosie's baby, we worked together. When it became obvious what Mrs. Burrough was doing to the girls, Francine and I agreed New Hope Mission had to include those babies. This was our plan, but actually finding James has changed much. Francine was first to decide what to do, and her decision didn't include me. I can't blame her for wanting to leave the property where death and dying was so prevalent. We will talk soon, I am sure, but I truly do not know what outcome this bodes for me. I walk into the entrance of what had been a boarded-up building, where I first encountered a shivering, scared and starving stray dog. The entrance has been remodeled the new marquee showcases NEW HOPE MISSION. I walk inside to a bevy of women making sense out of mayhem. The two weary doctors approach me, and we discuss the most urgent needs. My brain is taking it all in. My heart is warmed by this new reality, except I feel utterly alone. Francine is not here to share this with me.

———

SEAMUS WILL BE LEAVING for his work on the river in an hour. A light is on. We sent the carriage on its way with a generous tip. I knock on the door. Mary is holding James. We are here as much for Seamus and Rosie as we are for ourselves. A promise kept, a job well done and maybe, just maybe, to take in a sip of gratitude to quench a thirst of three years.

He opens the door warily. Then sees us holding a baby. The expression of shock gives way to elation. "You did it. Jaysus, Mary and Joseph, you did it!"

He is beaming. My cheeks are burning. Mary is crying happy tears, and James is sleeping.

"Where are my manners? Come in. Come in. Kettle is on. Tea?"

His parlor is neat. We sit. He prepares the cups and offers us the last of some fruit cake. I am famished, but I can eat later. I decline. He turns a kitchen chair around to face us and asks with equal measures of astonishment and admiration so many questions. Mary answers when she has direct knowledge, and I do the same. I do not gloss over how the girls were treated and what the constables dug out of the garden. His jaw drops when I tell him what spilled out of the armoire and how I found James alive and well. The conversation lasts well past the time he would normally head off to work, but eventually it winds down. I came with only one question on my mind, and he answered it without saying a word.

44

Three days have gone by since the discovery in the gardens. For the first time in months, Jack the Ripper does not captivate London as the lurid headlines and photographs of the foundling house and garden take center stage.

Parliament talks about making laws to regulate these houses. Chastity is espoused from the pulpits as a remedy for women having babies out of wedlock. No plans are made yet by the various denominations to provide housing or baby care for these women in need, but I can see the seeds are being planted for reform. Widows and orphans would have to make room for these women and children, and the sitting government sees it as a zero-sum game, arguing the rise in taxes is unwarranted.

I am somewhat of a hero in the circles of polite society. Lots of backslapping, brandy, and cigars at the club.

Meherhomji, Burrough and Felicity have all been charged with multiple murder counts, but Utterson assures me only Mary Burrough will hang. My friend and counselor has been aloof these past few days, and I am not sure why.

New Hope Mission is attracting donations from all over the world, from a few shillings to thousands of pounds. All of it is to go into the endowment fund.

The girls are responding as well as expected for babies withdrawing from opium and alcohol as we wean them off. Breast milk and sunlight are hugely helpful. All are making progress and gaining weight. Soon they will be ready for adoption. We have twice as many applicants as girls.

It's a dizzying time, yet the bed in the room next to my sleeping chambers goes unused. Lucky notices her absence too and whines at the door. Is she back with Seamus? A quiet inquiry at Mary McCreary's shop goes unanswered.

I am not worried about Francine's safety or for James O'Sullivan. She was self-reliant before I met her, and she would let nothing happen to the baby. I can't begin to describe what Francine and I have been through for the past couple of months, first with Jack the Ripper and now with Mary Burrough. How many mornings I stared at that green-eyed, red-haired, beautiful woman as she went about getting ready for a long and arduous day? How many private conversations over scones while sharing Lucky on the nights she returned from her forays into Whitechapel? If all I have left are memories, then those will be burned into my daily thoughts. I will see her in the babies' faces, English gardens, all things beautiful, always. I will see her in Lucy most of all. Utterson says the adoption paperwork is still across the Channel with Hanne's parents.

I miss Francine terribly, but there is much to do, and I am not sure if she will return. Will she go back to Whitechapel at night? Would Louise and Sally take over? So many questions, but for tonight exhaustion is taking over, and I am ready to retire when I hear a familiar knock on the door. It awakens Lucky, and he is bouncing up and down like my heart with excitement.

I fly to the door and fling it open. Francine stands there with a wide grin and says, "I have some Belgium chocolate for you. Would you like some?"

I sweep her into my arms and twirl her about. We laugh. Lucky wants to join in. We allow him. We laugh some more until we are dizzy and land backwards on my bed. Lucky gives her kisses and gives me a few more for good measure.

"I would have been home yesterday, but the ferry crossings from Antwerp were cancelled because of storms."

"Antwerp?"

"I met with your agent, and he took us to meet Hanne's parents. I told them we wanted to adopt the baby. I wanted them to meet me." They learned I was the last person to see their daughter alive and how brave she was to make sure the baby was going to be cared for."

"And?"

"They signed the papers relinquishing their rights. Lucy is ours, darling."

I am ecstatic. We are legally her parents, and Francine just called me darling, and she wasn't playacting. "And James?"

"Mary is bringing him over tomorrow."

"What about Seamus?" I ask.

"I am sorry I left you in such a rush. I wanted to show him I could find James. We first stopped to see Betsy Dwyer, the wet nurse, then I collected Mary and took James to meet his uncle before Seamus headed down to the river. We told him the entire story from beginning to end. Took us almost two hours, and during the entire time, he never once asked to hold the baby. Not once, Henry. That's what made my mind up." She pauses for a moment and reaches for my hand and places ours on her heart. "Two days ago, Utterson's man served Seamus with divorce papers, and I have been granted temporary custody of James until Rosie contacts us or abandons her rights.

"What can I say? We will be parenting Lucy, Edward and James if all goes well." I say.

"And the day my divorce comes through?" she asks.

"Will you marry me?" I ask.

She is coy. "Let's have some chocolate first, and no, Lucky, you can't have any."

EXCERPT: THE SEASON

BOOK 3

1

____

She's a dynamo; how am I ever to keep up with her? Springtime in Regency Park with light breezes from the west and the warm sunshine on my face promises a lovely April. My bride to be, Francine Murphy, and our maid, Lisbeth, are chasing our two little ones around me as I recline on the tartan picnic blanket. Our dog Lucky is joining in the fun. He loves the babies and is their protector here on the expansive lawns.

Children try to coax kites into flight, and they run themselves silly. Families with large wicker baskets produce many delicacies for a meal in the outdoors. Smoked fish. Spiraled hams. Finger sandwiches and many deserts. Dark-colored bottles for reds and clear bottles for whites. A pocket flask or two for a stronger nip, although there is no chilly wind to ward off on this unseasonably warm day.

I am happy to be taking in the scenery. Just walking here from Cavendish Square was tiring, but the women and toddlers are tireless. Francine and I are to marry as soon as her divorce is almost completed, and Lucy and James will legally become the children of Francine and Doctor Henry Jekyll.

In the two years and a half years since we first met, she has not slowed down. And me? Well, sometimes I pushed myself to my physical limits, but, truth be told, they have been fueled by my desire to be with her, to marvel at her feistiness and to feast my eyes on her beauty. I thought I was doomed to bachelorhood, having dealt my hand as a five-year-old. Now look at me, in love and with beautiful children.

However, I am more than twice her age, and as our world became more predictable and more stable, I find myself napping more often. My knees, elbows and shoulders complain loudly upon waking. But the minute I want to feel sorry for being ancient, I am reminded to be grateful for this remarkable woman who loves me without reservation and for these lovely little ones.

Lately, I have found myself at loose ends. Since my return from the West Indies, I have only visited my surgery occasionally. Once a respected doctor and chemist until my alter ego, Edward Hyde, beat to death our childhood tormenter, I retreated to the Islands to rid myself forever of Hyde. My practice was put on hold. I thought the herbalists and witch doctors were successful in banishing Hyde, but it was a good thing they weren't. Upon my return to proper London society, I had hoped to return to my practice, but then I met Francine and my life began changing for the better.

"Daddy, catch me!" James launches into the air, and my flabby stomach muscles scream in protest when my elbows stop supporting my fleshy frame. I reach out in time and dangle his belly inches from my lips. He laughs as I plant a dozen baby kisses on his tummy.

Not to be outdone, Lucy jumps on my back, and we sway back and forth. James tries to escape my grasp, and that's when my lower back twinges and I fall to my left side. Both children think it's part of the game, but I am seeing stars from the pain now radiating into my buttocks. Francine sees my dilemma and distracts the little ones long enough for me to turn onto my back.

Blue sky and puffy clouds finally replace the meteors shooting across my eyeballs. It hurts to breathe, and I pant like our dog until my spine settles and the muscle spasms recede. Lucky licks my face to take away the pain.

"Are you alright, darling?" She asks between giggles.

"Is it too late to not adopt these Chinese acrobats?" I smile through gritted teeth.

"I'm afraid it is too late, Henry." She bends down with a laughing, squirming toddler in each arm and plants a kiss on my forehead. "Just think how nice the bath will feel tonight."

"Shall I wait until you come home?" I ask. If the weather is fair, she will cab to Whitechapel, where she will walk about and talk with the women of the night who are selling their bodies for gin. All women have a past, but it is the future Francine sees in them that sends her out to the fetid, foul-smelling streets and alleyways.

With a sly wink, she says, "Don't you always?"

I nod as Lucky curls up next to me. I doze off sometimes when she is tardy returning to our West End manse, especially on the nights when she has to stop at the Mission. Her forays into Whitechapel are part of her identity as 'the do-gooder.' It would be easier for me to stop doctoring than what she does. She is driven by her own past, and now she is living her future, and she has never been more radiant. Living in the West End hasn't changed her, though. She knows that when she is talking with the ladies, she is not talking down to them. The devil once held her by the throat. Her thirst was for whiskey.

Lucky falls asleep next to me as my breathing becomes more even. Francine and Lisbeth take Lucy and James for a long walk around the ponds. I was probably snoring when my pooch awakened me with joyous barks signaling their return. Would I have enjoyed walking with them? Probably. Did I need to rest my back? Definitely. I stand gingerly on unsteady legs, not wanting to invite further back spasms. Am I becoming a softer version of myself, or is it the aging process? Neither option is acceptable as I watch my young family approaching. I shudder at the thought of approaching seventy years of age before my babies become adults. My body failing me is not part of the plan, and I need to do something about it. I stopped wishing I was twenty years younger when I met Francine, reminding myself, she would have been seven years old.

I tether Lucky to his lead, and Francine and Lisbeth place our protesting charges in their baby carriages. We walk back towards our home. Our home. Babies, Francine, the man who never thought he would find happiness. The man with a fractured past. To passersby, we are the well-to-do couple out for a springtime stroll after a long and cold winter. Once out of the park, I spy a carriage. I point it out to Francine.

"Go," she says. She takes the lead from me and gives me a kiss on the cheek.

I hail a cab and ask the driver for help. "Pulled a muscle," I say. I am a larger man, and it takes some doing to get me up the steps.

I settle into the soft leather seat facing forward and curse this predicament. Is this a harbinger of what is coming? What if Francine wants to have a baby of her own again? Will I have the stamina for yet another child? How am I to live these last chapters of my life? Francine and I have been through much. We are closer because of the adversity. We have stood together during perilous moments and have survived, but now that the excitement of our adventures has bled off, can we find joy in the mundane? Can we raise our babies and go about our lives and find fulfillment in the plans we made for ourselves?

Presently, I care for infants, and I help wean young women from the grip of gin, but what about the rest of my practice? I was once a respected doctor in this part of London. Is this unfinished business for me? Are there opportunities for me to be more than the source of money for the Mission? Purposeful work? Seeing patients again? Creating remedies for the ills of inhabitants living nearby? Why can't I start over? What is to stop me? Doctor Henry Jekyll, respected physician.

As I bounce and jostle over the cobblestone streets, my back reminds I am not getting any younger. Maybe a renewed purpose in what I studied and trained for will re-energize me.

The driver helps me from the carriage. Each step up into my front door entrance reminds me to eat less and exercise more. I try to remember the Greek or Latin for Physician, heal thyself and fail.

I hear Lucky barking in the distance. He sees me and cannot wait to rejoin his master. It is as if I was lost and now I am found. The dog Edward Hyde rescued reminds me to find myself again. I wave to everything I love and care about. The babies are fast asleep as the rosy-cheeked women smile in my direction. I am blessed, but I need to get off my feet.

ALSO BY JOHN A. HODA

Victorian-Era Mystery

Hyde and Seek

The Foundling House

FBI Agent Marsha O'Shea

Odessa on the Delaware: Introducing FBI Agent Marsha O'Shea

Clearwater Blues

Detroit Wheels

West Reading Traffick

Elm City Towers

Liberty City Nights, an FBI agent Marsha O'Shea prequel novella

Gwendolyn Strong Small Town Cozy Mysteries

Milford Elementary

Milford Coal & Ice

Milford Daffy Day

Milford Bed & Breakfast

ABOUT THE AUTHOR

John A. Hoda is an award-winning author and headline-making investigator. Readers applaud the realism and gritty dialogue he delivers from his work on the mean streets for the past five decades. He was the show runner of My Favorite Detective Stories podcast. John is a former insurance fraud investigator and police officer.

Hoda graduated from Indiana Univ. of PA with a degree in criminology. He moderates a writing craft study group and is an active member of the Fairfield Scribes, a critique group on steroids. John was a judge in the Shamus awards in 2019.

John has written the six-book FBI agent Marsha O'Shea police procedural series about a badass female agent trying to get her mojo back.

Mr. Hoda released his Gwendolyn Strong four-book small town traditional cozy mystery series in the fall of 2022.

He has written four how-2 books on the business side of running an investigations firm.

The podcast is heard in 79 countries with over 50,000 downloads. He interviews best-selling and award-winning authors about what makes their flawed fictional detectives tick.

He can be reached at hodagen@gmail.com.

Become an email subscriber for upcoming announcements at www.johnhoda.com